The Wayward

Wife

A Novel

By T. S. Wallace

The Write Way

Baltimore, Maryland 21217

Library of Congress Control Number: 2015905396

Fiction/African American/Contemporary Women

ISBN: 978-0-692-41769-0

ISBN: (10) 0692417699

This book is dedicated to the
"Women of the Well"
who want to get love right, but first
have to know, honor and love the God
within.

Acknowledgements from My Heart

This book would not exist had it not been for the friends who read it in all of its many forms, my literary group; Charm City Writers and its torchbearer Roslyn Alderman, and others too numerous to name, but whose ears I burned up with questions and who I reached out to for feedback. I thank them for their patience and thoughtful feedback. To my dear children, Tihira and Joseph, who put up with my crabby writing mood with patience, even in being served dinner late and burned pots smoking up the house from my getting lost in the lives of the people on these pages! I love you and this is for you to know your dreams are real and doable. I want to especially thank my friend – Sheri Booker, who told me not to give up and pushed me to not only complete my book, but to acknowledge and cherish my gift. I thank you all!

Accolades for The Wayward Wife

"The Wayward Wife is an unconventionally classic tale of a spiritual woman who finds herself embattled with her spirit (morals) and her flesh. This story exposes the reality that many women face. It will connect to women of all ages and invoke real discussions about the challenges married women face in their daily lives." **– Lanise Stevenson, Founder of the non-profit I Am Enough and DC Educator**

"I feel as though I am watching a movie! The story line is so different from what I expected. What I am enjoying most about it is the callous sexual acts juxtaposed with the morals and values of the characters. Often we get caught up with judging folks without knowing their story." **– Donna Bell**

"This is the type of book that makes you pour out your heart - It brought out so many emotions! Reading this story made me have to re-evaluate some things in my life and everyone can have a text to self-connection with this one. It was an easy read, there were no parts that dragged and everything was interconnected!" **– Nafeesah Burke, NYC Educator**

"Sin will take you farther than you want to go, keep you longer than you want to stay and cost you more than you want to pay."
-   Min. Ravi Zacharias

Why, my son, be intoxicated with another man's wife? Why embrace the bosom of a wayward woman?
- Proverbs 5:20

PROLOGUE

Jon called leaving me a frantic message: "*Neene!* I have been calling you for over half an hour! The office said you are gone on Wednesday afternoons for at least two hours and they couldn't reach you. This is my fifth call… Come to University Hospital as soon as you get this message. JD's been in a terrible accident." He whispered the last sentence as if saying it any louder would make it more real.

I was in the gym's shower when he called, removing traces of lust, getting my head together to return to the land of the righteous. When I heard what'd happened to my son, shame overwhelmed me. By the time I arrived at the emergency room, there was no time to wallow in my humiliation. The stark walls and piney disinfectant blinded my senses; numbness washed over me. I was underwater; seeing nurses' lips moving, but sound escaped me. I watched those white-coated messengers of doom come toward me, but the last thing I remember was the nightmare of Robert's face, then darkness…

I awoke from my dead faint with a nurse waking me, syringe in hand. I read her nametag and asked perplexed, "Ms. Marjorie, what is going on here?"

"Oh – Great! You are back with us. I can understand your being overwhelmed… How are you feeling now? Would you like something to drink?" She asked as she sat the syringe down on the table next to the bed and poured me a little paper cup of orange juice from a small white plastic container.

"I don't know… I mean… No. Did I just faint?" I asked, my eyes wide. I could feel my brows scrunch up.

"Yes…" She stated as she took out a penlight and shined it into my eyes.

"I checked your vitals and everything seems okay, so I was getting ready to take a small blood sample while you slept. We usually don't do that, but we are desperate." She continued slowly, looking me over and checking my vitals again.

"What? Desperate for my blood? Why?" I inquired while simultaneously trying to wrap my head around the scene that lay before me. Jon looked concerned and Robert was just staring at me, his thick eyebrows furrowed intensely. The room seemed void of the usual hospital staff, doctors and nurses buzzing about, which was strange and surreal. Jarringly, Nurse Marjorie broke into my thoughts of why that was, while I sipped from my paper cup becoming more alarmed by the second.

"Mrs. Dupont, your son needs multiple transfusions that will surpass our supply of his blood type by tomorrow, so we need to take some blood for testing. We are taking blood from your husband, you, as well as Mr. Matthews who so graciously volunteered to donate," she said almost too happily. *'God help me! Am I tripping? It's probably me; let me calm my nerves.'* I said silently.

"It will take at least 24 hours or so for us to know who matches, but we will use what reserves we have of his blood type in the meantime," Nurse Marjorie said with a smile.

"Of course. Thank you so very much," I said tersely, wondering what "Miss A Little Too Happy" could expose with this whole blood work scenario. All my business could be in the street in a matter of hours. I turned to face my husband and Robert, trying to gain my composure, failing completely.

"Well, R-R-Robert, H-Hi, umm… How have you been?" I stuttered thinking back to my dead faint at seeing his face. Maybe Robert felt like we *all* were such good friends at one time, it was only right for him to assist us in our time of need, but knowing his ass, probably not.

10

"I've been fine, Neene. Your son is a beautiful kid. I know he plays sports?" Robert said with a grin in his voice.

"Yes, JD plays basketball." I wanted to add, *Just like Jon,* but instead smiled to mask my sarcastic tone. *'Where was he going with all this?'* I thought to myself.

"Neene, I had just met up with Robert when I got the call, so he came along to support me. I was a wreck, so he drove," Jon said, trying to stop the drama he could see coming. He thought I didn't like Robert because of his reputation back when we were younger, if he only knew.

"I can understand why. It was hard for me to drive here alone myself…" I started shaking my head and thinking back to my journey to the hospital, tears filling my voice. "…Vision so blurry from crying, had to pull over and call Mishie… Told her JD was in a car crash, we cried, and then we prayed for the best together. That got me back on the road. Lord! I feel so horrible for not answering my phone!" I began sobbing uncontrollably.

"It's okay baby, come here; it's okay. You're here now," Jon said as he pulled me close to him and brushed my hairline with his mouth. "I was getting paranoid thinking maybe you had been in an accident yourself! I was so glad when you got here in one piece, but you scared the crap out of me with your fainting like that! Are you alright?"

"Yes, honey. I think I'm just drained from that workout and then the trauma of hearing about JD. Have you seen him? Is he awake yet?" I asked quickly hopping up off the gurney and reaching for Jon leading him towards Jon Jr.'s room.

"I looked in on him, but he's not awake yet," Jon said, stopping me just outside the room. "Baby, he is in an induced coma… Because of the loss of his foot," he said quietly into the top of my head.

"*What?*" I allowed tears to flow down my face unchecked as Jon pulled me close allowing my sobs to drench his baby-blue button down. Rubbing my back and murmuring softly, he held me letting the torrent pass. All I could think about was JD's dreams of NBA super stardom horribly destroyed.

"I think… I'm going to go ahead and leave now," Robert said clearly uncomfortable. "Okay, Jon?"

"Sure," Jon stated over my head. "Don't forget that we need to meet next week, aight?"

"Got it man. Don't hesitate to call me if you need me anytime, day or night. Neene, I pray everything works out for your son babe."

"Thank you for offering to donate blood for Jon Jr., Robert. Hopefully, his recovery will be swift and we will all be able to go out to dinner and talk about better times," I said quietly without moving my face from Jon's chest. It was safe there.

Jon and I turned to go into JD's room to talk to the doctors assembled there to find out what our next steps would be. Walking into the room, I instantly felt claustrophobic, there were three doctors crowded around his bed, one examining his leg, another perusing his chart and yet another watching us walk into the room. One started to speak, but I was completely oblivious.

"Jon's progress is great at this time. We are sure that he will recover nicely and we have the best rehabilitation specialist in Atlanta, Kirk Jones, lined up for him upon his release in a few weeks," the doctor who was watching us started hurriedly. I guess she could see the shock on my face, but didn't know I mentally checked out; I didn't hear a word she said.

I was focused on my beautiful boy; he lay there, scratches and cuts from pulverized glass imbedded into his smooth café au lait face. His barely out of adolescence build, tall and gangly just like my dad at his age, seemed wrong without the other size 11 foot resting near the one he still had. Right arm in a cast and his face swollen, I wanted to rush to his side, rub his curly 'fro and tell him it would be all right like I'd done when he was a toddler.

But aside from the assemblage at his bedside blocking my approach, I knew that things would never be the same. I snapped back from my internal thoughts, blinking and trying to focus, realizing that the doctors were telling Jon and I about JD's condition and release.

"My name is Dr. Kennedy and I am the orthopedic surgeon who is working with your son. I understand this is a trying time Mrs. Dupont, but I need you to understand what is going on so that you can care for your son upon his release," she stated while touching my arm and looking directly into my face to make sure she had my attention. I was still staring at JD out of the corner of my eye, but this time I heard every word.

"I'm listening doctor," I whispered.

"Good." She stated staring directly into my eyes and maintaining eye contact. "He is going to wake up out of the induced coma sometime tomorrow and we want you guys to be the first faces he sees. Do you have other children?"

"Yes," we said simultaneously.

"Well… Can there be some arrangements made for their care while you two hold vigil at his bedside?

"Their Godfather is going to pick up Amber and take her home with him. She should be fine there with her God-sister and brother."

"Great. That will give you some time to focus on your son, for a little while at least. He is going to need you guys to get him through this. I have seen cases where the person who loses a limb or extremity falls into a deep depression and never recovers so we are going to try to bypass that by having you both here, showing him that you support and love him unconditionally. What do you think?"

"We are committed to doing whatever it takes to make sure our son does not feel like he is less than who he was before this accident," Jon said emphatically.

"I would also suggest that none of his friends from school come to the hospital at this time unless he specifically requests them and he really wants to see them. Jon is a senior right?"

"Yes, he is." I replied, while Jon said, "Okay," simultaneously.

The doctor smiled at us and said, "Folks, I know this is a lot to take in all at once... We will make sure that Jon not only gets the best care available, but that we support you both in any way we can. If you need it, the chapel is on the third floor and a chaplain is on duty if you need him from 6 AM to 8 PM."

"Thanks doctor. We'll head there a lil later."

We decided to spend the night in the hospital and Jon would take the first shift while I ran home, got some clothing for us for a few days, checked on Amber and got us some food from his favorite soul food spot. When I returned, I saw Jon at JD's bedside, grimacing in his sleep from the weight of the world on his shoulders. I just watched him for a moment while I silently prayed that all I have done in the past 18 years wouldn't come crashing down around us both.

"Jon, honey... Want something to eat?" I said as I gently touched his shoulder.

Jon jerked like he had been electrocuted, but when he saw the startled look on my face said, "Oh! Damn baby... Didn't mean to scare you. I was having a bad dream, but now that I am awake, I see it wasn't a dream. Man... Baby, I know JD wasn't driving distracted and he was by himself, so I'm just wondering how he could have run the light and gotten hit by that truck! He's such a great driver."

"I don't get it either Jon. Where did the accident happen?"

"It happened somewhere near Prime Town Center. The doctor said it was sometime between noon and one o'clock this afternoon."

"What was he doing down there at that time? He should have been in school, right? I know today wasn't a half day – was it? Did he have his internship interview

14

today?" I asked. Something didn't add up, not only was I down there at that same exact time, I knew for sure that he didn't have a half-day.

"We can figure out all of that later. Right now, let's pray over our son."

"You are so right, honey." I acquiesced immediately loving how much my husband loved God and knew what to do at this time. God knew I needed a private conference with Him right then, but I would have to keep that to myself.

We took each other's hands, bowed our heads and Jon began to pray, "Father God, we come to you this evening saying thank you. Thank you for things being as well as they are right now God because this could have gone another way today God and we would be making arrangements instead looking into our son's face. We come now Father, in need of your mighty hand to touch our son. Father, touch his spirit, touch his mind, and guide the doctor's hands so that they can heal him in Your way Jehovah Raffa, which is a complete healing that only you can provide. God we come humbly through Your son Christ..."

As he prayed, I went over the day in my head, wondering how it could all have gone so wrong. While he prayed for our son's swift recovery, I prayed that my scandalous behavior hadn't culminated in my son's demise.

Jon finished praying and noticing the tears on my face, he wiped them saying, "Honey, don't worry. Whatever lies ahead, we can face it and overcome it, together."

Inside, I cringed. I just hoped that he would find it in his heart to forgive me if the need arose. God knows I have forgiven him for enough. We spent the night on that rickety hospital issued cot, spooned together, feeling like survivors of the Titanic; clinging to each other for safety and sanity's sake.

The next morning we awoke and went to the hospital cafe for breakfast. When we returned with our coffee, Lil' Miss Happy - Nurse Marjorie greeted us.

"Good Morning, Mrs. Dupont. Mr. Dupont," Nurse Marjorie nodded towards Jon, slowly walked close to me then furtively asked, "Do you know your blood type Mrs. Dupont?"

"Yes, My blood type is B negative. We donate blood to the Red Cross at my job twice a year," I said a little put off by how close she had gotten to me.

"B negative? Are you sure? I only ask because your husband's blood type is AB, which doesn't match with your son's blood type, which is 0 positive. I thought perhaps we had made a mistake with processing..." her rambling trailed off.

It felt like the air was sucked out of the room. I looked around rapidly, eyes bouncing off the walls, avoiding Jon's at all costs while blinking back tears that I hoped they thought were circumstantial.

Meanwhile, a perturbed Nurse Marjorie tried to take the blame, stating, "We tend to rush with ICU cases and things get mixed up, so let's not..." but couldn't downplay the meaning of this new fact. Neither of us matched.

CHAPTER 1

Janine: The Session

I sat in the doctor's office feeling bewildered; sure I looked confused, perhaps even upset to be there. I'd procrastinated in my navy blue Lexus truck in that barren parking lot at high noon, for what seemed like an eternity. I alternately stared in my driver's mirror studying my face and peered at this business card Jon had given me once he made my appointment. It read: Dr. Latasha Williams, LCPC & PhD Relationship Therapist specializing in Sexual Dysfunction and Marriage & Family Counseling, stenciled in gold calligraphy. I looked back into the mirror and saw the barely middle-aged married woman I am, but as I stared into my honey eyes, then habitually checked for gray in my reddish-brown hair, I hardly felt the part. Especially in light of all that has happened in the last three weeks.

      I smeared on some coral lipstick, turned off the car and started towards the door to the business park's offices thinking about the ultimatum I received from Jon last night at the hospital. We found out that JD would finally be released from the ICU and admitted to the rehab facility for three weeks before coming home, but I was robbed of my elation prematurely.

As soon as Dr. Kennedy left the room with the good news, Jon looked me square in the eyes with clenched teeth, and his jaw jumping furiously, told me, "If you don't go to that appointment tomorrow, I am packing our things and you will never see me or *your children* again."

Thankful that JD was still slumbering deep with the medication he was given, I didn't know whether to kiss Jon for forcing me to face my demons or smack his face for having the audacity to say something so outlandish to me. *'Take* my kids*! He has got to be joking or smoking,'* I thought to myself, then I smiled as if he'd said I looked lovely and replied sarcastically, "Why Jon, what makes you think I would do that?"

He just gave me a, "B#!ch please," look and slumped in the chair next to my son's bed, spent. We'd been in the hospital for three weeks rotating schedules, but in this rare moment of being here together, we were in a mental mine field just waiting for the other to make the wrong move so one of us could explode. I felt a myriad of splintered emotions all at once; loss, sorrow, gratefulness, relief, but apprehension tied them all together. That I'd decided at the last minute to come to this appointment at all showed I thought he was serious. Though in some ways I wanted to run screaming from this office, I also wanted to share what had been bottled up for so long with someone who was paid good money not to judge me.

"Well, you're here Janine", said Dr. Williams leadingly, "so the question becomes - are you going to share what brought you to my office or are we both going to sit here staring at my decor?"

I'd been just sitting there; like a deaf mute, thinking and looking around, taking in the dark paneled walnut desk, her plaques and degrees on the wall, the pictures of her husband or brother alongside them in golden frames that shimmered in the early afternoon sun streaming in through the large windows. I sunk deep into my seat admiring her taste; the toffee colored leather chaise and chair she had for her clients and the ethnic figures and carvings strewn about in chic fashion were exquisite! If she didn't have skills, she definitely had style. When I figured I had procrastinated enough, I took a deep breath and finally began to talk.

"Dr. Williams, please call me Neene. I just don't know if I can really tell you what happened specifically that brought me to this place; my husband gave me an ultimatum and if I didn't love him and my children, I wouldn't have even bothered to come."

"You know what I say?" she asked.

"No, what?" I replied mildly interested.

"If you don't really know where to start, start at the very beginning. The beginning of the affair or perhaps with your first connection to sex itself," suggested Dr. Williams.

"Well, the beginning of the affair that brought me to you is clear, and the beginning of my infatuation with sex is easy – I can't remember when I didn't know how good it felt. That sticky wet place where my thighs met always thumped and throbbed. I didn't associate it with boys until much later, after I touched and tasted it myself. Laying on my stomach and squeezing my thighs together tightly, ankles intertwined, holding my breath until the world disappeared and my heartbeat was one with the pulsation between my legs, became a favorite pastime of mine."

"It seems your sexual exploration started with you", stated the doctor as she took notes rapidly on her yellow legal pad, "do you still masturbate?"

"Yes, but it doesn't feel quite the same anymore after what happened once while I was orgasmic and oblivious as a little girl. I always expect to be caught and

feel guilty after pleasing myself, but I do it anyway...
There's nothing like knowing yourself intimately," I
chuckled softly.

"Tell me more about that," said Dr. Williams,
slowly, yet failing to hide her excitement as she inched
closer to the edge of her seat and leaned in ever so
slightly. I could tell she was eager to find out, but didn't
want me to know how interested she was in what
transpired while I was on the verge of bliss as a tender
prepubescent girl.

I obliged her curiosity by recalling quietly, "I
remember a boy cousin of mine finding me in my
masturbation position; lying on my stomach, hand
between my tightly clenched legs and climbing on top of
me. I felt his hardness pressed against me throbbing
against my taut behind, but don't even remember him
entering the room, I was so intent on feeling that freeing
sensation where stars burst behind my eyelids and the
world disappeared. His banana flavored Now or Later
breath, laced with more than just ganja, was hot in my ear
as he rotated his pelvis into my small catholic school plaid
clad frame. He ground me into that brown comforter
rhythmically for about ten minutes; I was so shocked and
scared I couldn't say or do anything. Then all of a sudden,
he said "Shit!" Jumped up and ran out of the room before
I could look up and see his face. He never uttered more
than that word, so I was unsure of which cousin it was
until I peeped his crisp white shell toe Adidas with the
red, green and black fat laces as he hit the door – Craig!
But I was still lost in my own wave after wave of orgasm."

"Did you ever tell anyone what your cousin did?"

I felt like I was being put on the spot because I
never did tell anyone specifically what had transpired. I
mean I was masturbating, right? Did I ask for it? Nobody
had talked to me about sex, my body or the sensations I
felt when alone, but I somehow got the feeling from
those older and in charge of me that masturbation and sex
was not a good thing. I wasn't sure how my mother or my

aunt would perceive it and I for damn sure didn't want to tell my father! I was unsure of how to answer her. I sat forward allowing my hair to cover my face for a moment while I thought. I sat up, tucked it behind my ears, and I decided to tell her what happened when I recently attempted to share it with my cousin Janis.

"I recently mentioned to a cousin of mine that he may have done something inappropriate to me when something came up about his drug abuse back then. You know, crack was new then and people didn't know how bad it would be in the early 80's, but Janis said I shouldn't mention it to anyone else because it was so long ago that it didn't matter anymore."

The doctor clicked her tongue and said, "Humph – How did you feel when Janis said that?"

"I felt like I didn't matter to anyone who should love me and care for me, if she felt like that! I also felt that my safety was of no concern." When I said that, and let how I really felt actually surface after over five years of telling someone; it all came flooding back – the shame I felt after I told my cousin what happened, the feelings of being on my own without anyone to really look out for me as a child. I did not say this to the doctor, instead what I did say was, "Doctor, I was left alone so much as a child I may have well been raising myself. I was a solitary, shy child – the 'bridge-baby', with 7 years between me and any other cousin. I was left finding ways to enjoy my own company quite frequently."

"How did being left alone frequently make you feel?"

"I didn't know any better so I didn't feel anyway about it really. I loved reading so I had lots of time to indulge a favorite pastime. I know I loved being left alone in my own house for sure. We lived in the penthouse apartment of a corner brownstone on 123rd Street and Manhattan Ave. My father and his friends renovated the apartment to suit my mother's wishes before the talk of divorce started; there were the prerequisite hard wood floors, exposed glossy red brick and an open floor plan that people are so fond of now. She made them put in a large hardwood loft that partially covered the living room and was the perfect hiding place! They knocked down the kitchen wall and put in an island too – Joleene knew exactly what she wanted – that woman had style and vision before her time! We had African art all over the walls, Kente clothe hangings and a booming sound system that I blasted Diana Ross and Alexander O'Neal on when no one was home. I loved it without even knowing that it was much different from anyone else's house.

"Before the talk of divorce?" Broke in the doctor... "Hmm, what was the divorce talk like between your parents?" She added.

"I don't know doctor. I don't even know why I said that..." I said trying to evade her question. My parents arguing and name calling and ultimately their split was akin to a tape player on repeat that was always in the back of my mind somewhere.

"We'll come back to that later," stated the doctor, almost to herself, as she jotted something new down in her legal pad and leaned back in her seat. "Tell me more about where you lived and growing up."

"Well, even my best-friend Michelle's apartment, which was on the second floor of that brownstone, was tricked out. Michelle and I used to hang out practicing tongue kissing in our tar beach hideout, it was surreal; the sun made the tar gummy beneath our Pro-Keds and we would sit in one place along the roof line so long we would be stuck! She always tasted like the spicy sweet tamarind balls I brought back to her from my trips to Franklin Ave visiting my cousins. We used to play up there on the roof all summer long talking about boys and how much we hated them but wanted to kiss them anyway, while playing with our Barbie dollhouses - making Ken take out the garbage and mow the fake lawn. Our tar-beach was fun!"

"Wait a minute!" The doctor cut in abruptly, "did you say your first experience outside yourself sexually was with your best friend? A female best friend?"

I chuckled, because instead of her responding to us playing on the roof of a brownstone in the middle of Harlem, she was more concerned with our sexual experimentation, but this was sex therapy right?

"Yes, Dr. Williams, I kissed a girl. And I guess I liked it because my best friend Michelle and I practiced kissing each other the summer she and I turned 12. Neither of us liked boys too tough, so we decided that until they would act right, we could practice on each other. We were trying to get the turn of the head and the position of the nose thing down pat."

As she sat there mulling over what I said, in her pale flesh colored silk blouse and deep purple skirt, I realized Dr. Williams was an attractive young woman. She let one purple Manolo Blanik shoe dangle from her stocking clad foot using her tortoise shell eyeglasses to push her long bob out of her face as she took notes. She finally looked up, her small coffee bean eyes snared me and she said, "Okay Neene. Hmm… When was your first male sexual encounter?"

CHAPTER 2

Janine:

My Love, My Frustration

"My first real sexual encounter with a boy was quite a few years later, when I seduced my first boyfriend Jesus. He was the cutest boy I had ever seen; in winter he was brown lightly toasted Wonder bread, but he would match my caramel in the summer sun. He had this low-cut, curly Afro that I loved to run my hands in when we kissed for hours on end. I remember I use to tease him about putting gel in it every day. He was always brooding - looking all serious and dangerous – always loved the bad boys! I know he was involved in some illegal activities but I didn't care, it made him more attractive to me because of my catholic schoolgirl upbringing. He took Karate and was a golden gloves boxer, so he was sculpted like an athlete; forget six-pack, he had an eight pack! When we stood face to face, my face was at his neck so he wasn't very tall but he was the perfect size for me."

"What kind of illegal activities did you think he was involved in Neene? Were you at any point afraid of him or what he did? Do you think it was a good idea to date someone like him?" Dr. Williams began peppering me with questions like rapid machine gun fire.

"Doctor Williams, this was Harlem in the 1980's! Crack was *king* and even if your boyfriend wasn't involved, he was involved, because his friends were. I actually think he was a hit man because he kept it really low-key, but was always strapped. He wasn't flashy or violent with me, but he always had money in his pocket and got my hair and nails done every week. To put it plainly, it was the norm. I was a "good girl," my parents worked and took very good care of me. Shoot – they bought me a fur coat when I was 16 years old! I also worked as a cashier in Gristede's midtown, so I always looked good with or without a boyfriend. I think that is why I was able to hold out so long before giving him any to begin with. Please doctor, you have no idea, I knew girls in junior high school who were selling themselves like prostitutes for 54.11's and Parasuco's on a regular!"

Doctor Williams sat there looking dumbfounded making me wonder if she was really ready for all I had to share. I didn't want to overwhelm the one person I felt might be able to give me an unbiased viewpoint and perhaps some advice on what to do about my current situation. I decided to continue with the story and let her stop me if she needed to.

"Okay so, Doc, I was 18, he was 18 going on 19 and had already graduated from high school the year before. We'd been dating and making out for almost three whole years – to the point where just looking at him made me wet and him stand at attention. After doing my homework, him doing his Golden Gloves calisthenics work out mixed with martial arts and a little bit of showing off, and us eating the Cuban food he made at his dining room table, we found ourselves intertwined for hours grinding to the 89' Kid Capri slow jam tape. This one night, we were in the room he shared with his little brother atop one another rolling around on his twin sized bed rubbing and touching each other kissing breathlessly. Fire and Desire blasted in the background from his boom-box on the floor, and my eyes kept wandering to the scantily clad Apollonia plastered all over his walls and I wondered how my 18 year-old body measured up in his mind. My standing up, faking like I was trying to get away from his assault, found me pressed against his low dark wood paneled dresser with our hands down each other's pants stroking each other almost to climax. His cologne bottles clinked against his gel jar as we got into a rhythm, rubbing one another. I swear I can still hear them clink and feel his finger slick with my wetness pressing against my pearl and sliding the length of my center without entering. He was alive in my hand; veins pulsing, his pounding heartbeat made him thump, thump, thump against the strokes of my hand."

I had to pause for a moment and shake my head to clear the images from my mind to continue. When I looked at her, I caught her look away quickly back to her notepad and begin scribbling something, probably nonsensical bull – she was caught up in the story just like I was, so I just decided to keep going from where I left off.

"Standing at his dresser at dusk, oblivious to the hour except in how the summer sun's position made us glow golden deep orange, I couldn't stand it another second longer, I whispered, "Now," as I tore my mouth away from his and looked deep into his chinky mocha eyes. He asked me if I was sure sounding more afraid and surprised than I was. I pleaded, yes, please. But doctor, I really was scared to do it. I just felt like I didn't want to leave and go away to school without giving him what I had made him wait for so long." I broke into my own story because I felt like maybe I should explain why I would give in after holding out for so long. Plus, it was getting too good, I began to lose my focus a bit on why I was there!

"If you had waited, what did you think would have happened between you two?" asked Dr. Williams.

"I am not sure doctor, but back then I felt that this one young man, who on Saturday's sat in my mama's living room with me and my dad watching Kung Fu flicks for more weekends than I can count, knew me well. I thought that he knew I was afraid and had respectfully waited patiently for this moment, but my actions that early evening made him doubt I had never done the deed."

"He thought you weren't a virgin…" She stated leadingly.

I paused and began to reminisce about how it all went down… And said, "I guess it's because of how it happened; I wasn't afraid, I was eager." The entire story came flooding back like – Whoosh!

THE FIRST TIME

I coaxed him back to his baby blue crisp cotton sheets and pulled my t-shirt with my name graffitied "Neene" in brightly colored spray paint, over my head in one swift movement. He pulled his wife-beater over his head and pulled my already open Big John jeans down my narrow hips and over my thick thighs, inside out, casting them aside. As Rick James and Tina Marie belting out their undying love in "Fire and Desire" began to fade and Luther began to croon 'Don't you remember you told me you love me baby…' I watched him look at me as I lay back and removed my bra then slowly tugged my panties down. I reached for him, pulled him closer, slowly undid his army pants all the way and slid them down his slim flanks all the way off and pulled him in his boxers towards me. The room was aglow in a darkening blood orange scene as Jesus kneeled over me, my sandalwood vanilla musk and his dove clean scent intermingling, entranced me. He looked at me as if to say, "Are you sure baby?" And in reply, I reached up and tugged on his boxers, his eyes widened a bit then collapsed into even thinner slits as he dove down toward my mouth and kissed me; wet, warm, spicy and sweet like the plantains and arroz con pollo he cooked for our after school meal. He made his way down my body slowly, tasting every inch of the course. I giggled when he stuck his tongue in my innie, but moaned deep and low in my throat when I felt it on my pearl. His lips enclosed it and he tugged gently rubbing his tongue on it lightly; a greedy baby – he suckled my clitoris as if he hadn't been fed in weeks. My legs began to tremble uncontrollably and I could feel my juices begin to wet the sheets under me. I had no idea that this could feel so good, but I wanted more – I begged him to let me feel him inside me and he obliged. Oh my goodness, I have never had anything feel so electrifyingly pleasurable that hurt so badly simultaneously – exquisite pain. My squeal turned moan and made him be still inside me, but he pulsed rhythmically and we began to rock forth and back and back and forth, no stroking, just rocking as I stretched to accommodate him inside my secret space.

He held me tightly in his arms with his face and hands buried in my doobie, my mouth; slightly open, rested on his neck while my hands wrapped around his back, gripped the top of his shoulders, I wrapped my legs around his lean waist and we began to kiss, limbs intertwined for what seemed like hours. I began to feel the urge to move so I began to slowly grind my hips to the sound of the wind in the trees, as we never got up to turn the tape over. Jesus followed suit; slowly grinding in, out and around, stirring a building excitement inside me centered around a space between my belly button and the top of my mound. The excitement began spreading from where he sat inside me: a catalyst for the fire spreading through me. I became a river, liquid and gushing as we began to move faster to a rhythm in our hearts and loins beating in tune. Finally, I felt an explosion, as it seemed

Jesus stretched me further until we seemed part of the same flesh and the river within me gathered strength and flowed, filling me to overflow.

He lay atop me for a moment while we each collected our thoughts and became two again, looking at me quietly, Jesus kissed my forehead gently then said, "I love you, Neene", paused then added: "Your father's gonna kill us both if I don't get you home soon."

I looked into his eyes for a moment and slowly said, "Thank you for being so gentle 'Seus, I love you too and you're right, if we don't get back, Dad's gonna kill us," with a giggle.

After a semi-frantic search for our clothes in the dark that should have been late afternoon but was more like mid-evening, the shock of bright white tile in the sparkling bathroom, the icy white commode and the inferno between my legs were at odds all competing for my concentration. Losing that battle, I just closed my eyes and prayed, 'Please God, it felt so good, please don't let it hurt like this,' as my urine blazed a trail of wildfire in its escape. I used a white washcloth doused in frigid water to stop the erupting flames and sat locked in his 3rd floor project bathroom on the toilet, holding my cho-cha, afraid to go home in the dark.

I'd never told anyone about my first time, especially not in such detail! I had to take a deep breath and center myself to even be able look the doctor in the eyes again.

"Dr. Williams, they say it's never as good as the first time and I swear they are so right! Jesus and I broke up not long after that because although he said he loved me, because I had him wait so long, he had some other woman on the side – and this girl turns up pregnant right before I left to go away to Spelman! I couldn't believe it!"

"How did you feel when you found out? It seems you invested a lot of time and effort into that relationship – Neene," asked Dr. Williams.

"I felt betrayed and I think that's why I still think you should never trust a man, because whether they love you or not, it doesn't mean they won't stray," I said angrily.

"Really?" replied Dr. Williams, "Why then, did your husband, give you the ultimatum?" she challenged quietly.

"That's a whole 'nother situation doctor," I replied defensively, with a snap in my neck and a roll of my eyes. How dare she come at me like that? I guess the black on black Gucci bag, red-bottomed shoes, Prada glasses and the proper diction had her fooled! I am a well-educated Black woman, but I am also from Harlem!

"So Janine, how did we get to this place we are now?" asked Dr. Williams quietly.

"I always had a bad girl lurking deep inside me and she always came out when there was a man involved. I even gave her a nickname when I was younger – "Tonya". It sounded like a girl who knew her way around the block even if she hadn't quite been all the way around it, if you know what I mean – an "around the way girl" sounding kind of name you know Doc?" I laughed thinking of LL Cool J's song.

"Well, that is a common Black girl's name I will admit, although I wouldn't go so far as to say all the Tonya's 'know their way around the block' so to speak," Dr. Williams responded tactfully.

She must have a close friend or sister named Tonya, I laughed to myself and said, "Okay Dr. Williams, I concede. You're right, not all the Tonya's in the world are promiscuous, but it seemed like an anonymous name that could be any girl and every girl, making what I did when I played Tonya, harmless," I replied.

"Well, what kinds of things did you do when you 'played Tonya' Neene?" asked Dr. Williams innocently enough.

However, I wasn't sure how to answer this question. I was at a crossroads in establishing exactly why

I was sitting in this plush downtown Atlanta office spilling my guts to this prissy young chick. I wasn't sure if 'Miss Highbrow' could really relate to my history, although I was certain that there were thousands, if not millions of little girls out there, just like I was, right at that very second. God only knew what they were doing to fit in or to assuage that ache for love they feel, just like I did and sometimes still do.

I started by saying, "I had a few one-nighters doctor; it's not as if I was on a rampage or anything, not really anyway. That summer before I left for school was a blur though. It seemed like I stayed high on Chocolate Thai or tipsy from gin and juice – anything to numb the pain. Although I had just started having sex, it seemed like I needed more once we broke up for some reason, almost as if the sex I had with other men made Jesus' memory fade away – until I met Jon. He was the perfect gentleman and I met him right here in Atlanta at a Spelman/Morehouse after party at my job – Club 112. I also met his best friend Robert the same night.

CHAPTER 3
Jon: M.I.A.

Where the hell is she? I thought as I tried Janine's phone for the fourth time in the past hour. I decided not to take the long drive to work today after there was a pile up on the interstate; I just doubled back and came back home. I wanted to surprise her, but needed to know where she was to set it all up.

"*Damn!*" I had to stop take a deep breath and think, "Ok, I will leave her a message, maybe she left her phone at home and is at the gym or it's in her gym locker. Hmmm... I will give her another hour."

Deep in my heart, I knew she was doing something she had no business. I had been getting this nagging feeling lately that all was not right at home, but I just couldn't pinpoint where it started or what exactly triggered this suspicion. I settled into my drive home through the clogged thruway, thinking intently about when this feeling wasn't present. As I drove, I thought back to when I met Janine; it was at a Homecoming after party at Club 112 in Atlanta where she worked; I was a senior at Morehouse and she a junior at Spelman. I even remember what she had on; she looked like New York all the way – form fitting skinny acid wash Guess jeans that showed off her high round onion behind, crisp new purple Jordan high top sneakers, doorknocker earrings and a purple off the shoulder top with white and black graffiti on it – she was fly.

My man Robert saw her first, but when I laid eyes on her, I knew she was the one. Her lips were all shiny as she smiled talking to her clique, looking good enough to bite. Her girls, Michelle and Jasmine, all bust out laughing, 'cause she said something slick and funny, no doubt. You could tell she was the diva of the group because they all tried to emulate her style but with Levis and black 54.11s. They were all cute, well kind of… Michelle or Mishie as they called her, was short and petite with a shapely body, creamy caramel skin topped with a short Halle Berry hairstyle, but she reminded me of a Chihuahua with her sharp chin, pointy nose and small eyes. Jazzy-Jazz on the other hand was a statuesque, Amazonian young lady, possessing the epitome of a Coca-Cola bottle figure, a good looker with long, 'curly when wet', hair and sexy Spanish looks, she was definitely a candidate for tonight's activities. But that Janine, or Neene as they called her, man, she just did it for me immediately; her caramel skin, hazel eyes and how that doobie fell softly, right between her shoulder blades; she was perfect.

Robert and I both stood 6'3" but were night and day in looks and build; I'm dark skinned and Robert is the light skinned, curly hair type; shoot he and Janine coulda passed for fam back then! Where I was athletic and lean, he was husky and played football and of course, I played basketball. He was from Atlanta, me from Brooklyn, New York. Not to say we were polar opposites, because although we were different, we both loved the ladies, sports and wanted to be successful athletes and businessmen one day, so our competitive spirit and self-confidence on and off the field was matched. No man on campus could even touch our stats – with the ladies, on the field or on the court; we were the men to watch and best friends to boot. How'd Kanye say it? Our swagger was on a hundred thousand million! Robert already had a few scouts from the NFL on him as our star quarterback last season and the NFL had just revised their eligibility rules so as a new senior, Robert had renounced his college playing eligibility in order to go pro his senior year. He had money coming at him from four teams that were getting ready to be approved by the NFL to start but he had yet to make a decision, he said 'Let them all keep courting me! Sheeeet! I may just go play overseas until they get their shit together' all the time.'

  We sat there watching the women, peeping the haters watch the women watchin' us, and I told Robert, "You know that hottie Neene? I think I might wife her. She's the type I wanna cuff long-term."

  Robert looked at me, "Oh yeah? Well, we'll see if she likes chocolate or vanilla, 'cause I'm checkin' for her myself!"

  I chuckled to myself cause I knew where this was headed, and I was down for the game at the time. "Aight man, we shall see who she chooses by the end of the night – whoever she chooses tonight is the man too, no second tries later on – Deal?"

  Robert, staring at Neene and her crew headed our way, replied absently, "Yeah… I saw Janine first… But aight Jon… Here they come."

  That night was crazy! My homeboy Marcus joined us to even out the group cause he was diggin' Mishie and we wound up at Slice because they stayed open late for homecoming. It was this new hot spot that appealed to both Atlanta natives because of the down home customer service and the New Yorkers' because of the pizza and the vibe. It was mad hard to get 'real' pizza anywhere near campus! Pizza Hut and Dominoes delivered right to your door, unless you had the money to dine out and it was all you ate in terms of pizza, but it was nowhere near NY pizza, plus Slice didn't deliver!

How did I get that fly ass chick to not only leave the club with me, but to convince her home-girls to come along too? C'mon man, I was the man on campus! All the chicks knew about me and even though Janine was a junior and only dated off campus, she knew my rep from gossip and I knew hers – she liked the older scramblers dudes from the area: "bad boys". I was gonna make her see that "good boys" weren't so bad after all.

We danced to Biggie's *Give Me One More Chance Remix* with Total and started to talk she began realizing that not only was I from NY, but from Brooklyn and that I really loved home as much as she did! It was on from there! She was used to dealing with these slow ass bamma dudes she could wrap around her well-manicured pinky finger, but I was gonna prove to her that not only was I from home, I could rep New York to the fullest, without being outside the law.

As I ground my hardness into her firm onion to the rhythm of the bass, I asked her, "Where's your man Neene? Would he have a problem with us being this close on the dance floor?"

She turned toward me and spoke directly into my ear just loud enough for me to hear. "My man don't come on campus baby, I do me... then, I do him." She replied real sexy-like, then giggled like a little girl. "Nah, for real though, I am tired of dealing with hot bammas. I need a good man. I'm a junior now and I need to be with someone I can really BE with, you know..."

I knew exactly what she meant. I was feeling the same pull as a senior graduating in less than three months, that feeling where you feel like you need to stop playing and make the decision to be in a relationship that can go somewhere tangible. I wasn't thinking marriage exactly, but at least wanted to have the option if I felt like it.

I replied, "Well, baby you can BE with me anytime you want," turning her back towards me and placing my hands on her on waist. The DJ switched the song to Shabba Ranks – *"Girl fleeexxx ah, time to have sex ah…"* My thumbs almost met in that dip in the small of her back and I felt her arch ever so lightly in response making me instantly pulse against her backside. When she moved against me in return, I was surprised! Neene's attitude gave me the impression it would be so much harder to get her open like that. Then, I realized that she'd had a gold bottle of Pierre Jouet glued to her hand from when we spotted them at the door – she was wet, in more ways than one, by the way she rode me and the beat – dancehall queen winding her mango ripe ass on my stiff cane; she had me open. The usual slide off was my first thought as the song ended and I told her to come on, but as I watched her about to saunter off to tell her girls she was leaving, I reached out, grabbed her hand and said, "Neene, tell your girls to come with you. I'm gonna get my boys and we all gonna get somethin' to eat."

I guess I wanted to see what she was really about, plus I wanted to see if she would slide a lil more sober. It was about one in the morning anyway, so I figured everybody would be with it. Funny thing is, that morning when I called to check on her before class, she didn't answer the phone – I actually didn't speak to her again for about four months. And now that I think about it that was the first time she went AWOL.

"Let me think," I said to myself breaking out of my reminiscing, I am away from Wednesday night to Saturday every week. We have our date on Saturday and family outing and dinner on Sunday. That's our family's routine, but as the lead architect and co-owner of my firm, Wednesdays; or hump-day as it's called, are always mega-busy for me. We are in the middle of building green office space in an up-and-coming part of Charlotte and the contractors need to be watched carefully. Marcus' wife, Michelle is undergoing chemo, so I am the man for the job. We got the contract and the news about Michelle almost simultaneously; it was bittersweet. Marcus and I worked hard together to build this firm after graduating Morehouse together in 1991, at first it was crap jobs and long nights and sometimes we weren't only the architects we were the contractors as well, but the hard work and long nights we put in paid off! We're well off, our children and wives want for nothing. We proved our salt and once we got a few write-ups for building green and cheap – our business tripled. We made a couple kids; Junior came during our foundation phase – Neene's senior year, and we got married after her graduation.

We built our dream home in Sandy Springs in the same alcove as Marcus and Mishie. All that was missing was Robert, but he was in the midst of resurrecting himself after leaving the NFL with rumors of drug abuse following him like the plague and being incarcerated for possession of cocaine. He actually just started using his Morehouse degree in Business Management for something worthwhile; starting the Douglas Detective Agency. We had lost touch a while after graduation, but I got the news on him from Marcus from time to time. It was strange to me that he never got married or had a family. We used to get busy back in the days with the honeys, *shoot*! I laughed to myself; it was a competition.

"Almost home… Maybe I should swing by Mount Vernon Prep, pick up the kids and take them to an early dinner. Let me try Neene again first though." I thought, praying that she would answer the phone.

"Hey baby", she said sweetly after answering on the first ring.

"What's up Neene? I have been trying to get you on the horn all day! Where have you been?"

"Come on Jon, you know I meet with my personal trainer at Prime Town Center Gym." She said with a smile in her voice. Then, "What's up? Aren't you in Charlotte working on your project? Is everything ok? Y-y-y-you didn't get hurt did you?" she stammered quickly.

"Nah. I am about to pick the kids up, meet us at the mall for early dinner. I know I am coming right back unexpected, so I am not going to make you cook everything I like!" I said smiling.

She laughed, "Humph! If you thought I was, you were sadly mistaken! The kids and I go out every Wednesday evening, their choice, so you are right on time – pick them up, let me know where they want to eat and I will meet you all there. Is everything alright?" she asked again with concern in her voice.

"Everything's okay babygirl. There was a big accident on the interstate with a tractor-trailer and a few cars when I was only about an hour away from home. While I sat in traffic, I started thinking about this morning before I left…" I laughed. "…and I didn't want to go in anymore, I wanted to get it in like that again tonight; I miss you when I am away. So, I called in to the foreman to let him know I wouldn't be coming in."

"Oh really!" She said sounding really surprised. "You have never done that before… Are you sure everything is alright?"

It wasn't, but I didn't want her to know how not all right things were. So instead, I just said, "Baby everything is just fine, I love you. See you in a minute."

"Love you too," she replied.

As I hung up, I began to think about Sunday's service, Bishop was talking about Hosea and Gomer. Man! I pitied Hosea; everyone knows 'you can't make a hoe a housewife,' but God made him work that out! This whole not being able to find Neene mess, has me wondering if I made the same choice or if God led me to do the same thing. I remember leaving service that day feeling out of sorts. I mean if God ever called me to forgive my wife as he forgave the sinners of old – Who am I to deny Him? I didn't think I would be able to do it to be honest, but I gave praise and thanks to the Almighty that I didn't have to think about that in my situation. I'm also glad that what I do, will never interrupt my family life. That chicken-head Gomer was messing up their family in ways a man who cheats never can, but now that Neene had been MIA again, I am feeling like perhaps I may need to reevaluate how I see my wife…

Bishop preached about how the Israelites felt like God had stopped talking to them and that was why they went astray. They wanted something they could tangibly see and touch to worship and that was not how God operated; you had to go on faith in God, the knowing that he was there for you and not only had your best interests in mind, but also would never forsake you. They didn't know how God really worked or how love really worked, so they went astray. I sometimes feel like Janine doesn't understand why I am away so much, I want to make sure we never have to want for anything. Can't have my children grow up poor or needy like I did in BK.

My father worked damn hard as a contractor, to die a poor, broken man without a pension for his family to live on in his absence. I loved what my dad did so much, I followed in his footsteps, but I wanted to live my life right *and* have everything I wanted materially too. I thought she understood that with her father starting out as a struggling contractor as well, but now I have my doubts. She used to complain so much about missing me and needing my presence at home with her and the kids, but then the complaints just stopped. She hasn't changed how she treats me, but I'm going to have pay the Douglas Detective Agency a visit.

CHAPTER 4
Janine: Confessions

Dr. Williams said softly, "I know you are here because your husband has given you an ultimatum, but it has to be useful for you. I want you to think about what your goals are for these four individual sessions that we are having and what you want out of them. Later when your husband joins the sessions, he can share his goals as well."

"I want to love my husband the way he deserves," I stated deliberately.

"What do you think this change will entail on your behalf Janine?" Dr. Williams asked quietly. "What would be your first steps toward it?" she added.

"I don't know. I do know that I get extremely lonely when Jon is away on business; my work and girlfriends don't make that feeling go away. Shopping, eating out, working out and working at my shelter, none of it does for me what attention from a man can. When I am home in bed and the children are asleep, I need to lay with someone; feel their warmth pressed against me, keeping me safe and feeling loved."

The doctor nodded, urging me to continue my explanation.

"Take for instance the first night I met Jon. I met his best friend Robert that night as well. They had reps on campus as ladies' men who had it going on, but I had my own popularity intact, so I wasn't at all impressed, until I actually hung out with them. They rolled like the ballers I was used to dating, but they were college boys! They made me re-think how I was going about my dating life, to be honest. I was tired of dating the same old tired drug dealer with money and swagger, but no sense. I wanted to be able to talk about more than sex, fashion and music with my man. I wanted a man who was well read but had swagger and money, but that was a tall order. Then, when I saw Robert and Jon that night, it was like 'Ding! Pick it up!' I had found the Holy Grail of dating as a Black educated urbanite."

Dr. Williams broke in after shaking her head slowly, "We still have that problem almost twenty years later, so I can definitely identify with your plight, but how is this related to your needing a man to warm your bed at any cost?"

"Well, I don't know exactly, doctor, but I liked both of them. I didn't want to choose so, at first, I didn't. We all met at this hot party at my job; my girl Jazz was on Robert all night for show, she gave him my number and told him that I wanted to meet with him after we ate as soon as I realized that Jon was going to send me home with my panties wet. She had a boyfriend and she was not the type to stray. I wanted Robert out the gate, before they even approached us, he was in my sights – his curly hair and brawny body was calling me reminding of my first boyfriend Jesus so much, at first, looking at him made my heartbeat speed up and ache. But Jon was also attractive with his beautiful chocolate skin and deep-set eyes with those long eyelashes; I was so torn that when Jon and I danced to Shabba Ranks' *Flex*, I was dancing with him, but watching Robert like a hawk imagining it was him. The girls dragged me out to drink and be merry because I had broken up with my boyfriend - like three months prior with no new takers or prospects, so when we saw them, I was on the prowl."

"Do you mean rebound?" inserted Dr. Williams.

"No, I meant prowl." I said curtly. "I hadn't had any in over three months and I was on fire. Robert was throwing smoke signals while I danced with Jon, so I knew it could be on between he and I. Jon had me windin' on him like a dancehall queen, so I could imagine how good it was gonna be with him too, until then he pulled the "good boy" routine on me and was like. "Go get your girls". I was some kinda frustrated! I mean everyone knows you slide from the club, not from I-Hop!"

"So, how did you manage to have them both?" Dr. Williams asked wide-eyed like she was afraid to hear what I was going to say.

"Chile, I did *not* have a threesome with those two if that is what you are thinking! I had Robert first. Mary J Blige's *You Remind Me* was in my head every time I looked at Robert. I had to."

Clearly confused, Dr. Williams said, "I don't get it. How did you do that, when you were all out together? Did you think about anyone's feelings but your own? Did you consider Jon at all?"

"No. I didn't and I guess I never have. We had just met and I wasn't beholden to either one of them yet. I did what fit my purpose at the time and up until now, I didn't really think or care about anyone else's issues with what I do. I felt like I was doing what they wanted when I did what I wanted, if not, then – too bad for them. What I want takes precedent and that night, I wanted to be laid down by Robert. In retrospect, that may not have been the way to do things, but I was young; it was fun. I wanted and needed that from him at the time."

"What about now? Is it fun now? I am asking because I am wondering if your behavior has changed, perhaps I am wrong… but you just said 'What I want takes precedent' – meaning to me, this still holds true, what does it mean to you?" replied the Doctor quietly.

I was mortified that I had said that and even more so that she'd caught it! *'She is well worth the money Jon is shelling out for these sessions,'* I thought incredulously. I didn't know what to say. All I could think about was how Robert turned me out that night. I mean I had just lost my virginity about four years prior, had three boyfriends, including my first, Jesus, and a one-night-stand. They were okay in the bedroom, but I never had that 'Jesus' feeling with them sexually; drunk or sober, but with Robert that night, I experienced something I never had before or since, except with him. I can't even truthfully say I regret it, because even after all the drama, I still feel like that one night was worth it.

I finally replied, "That night was a blur, flashing lights, food, flirting and being tipsy was all we needed to get it popping, but even tipsy I could tell Jon was holding back… Watching me, wanting to see if I was easy or wifey material and I wanted to be a good girl for him, but Robert was watching me too and I wanted to be his nasty girl, wanted him to 'slap it, flip it and rub it down'."

Doctor Tasha looked confused, so I explained, "That was a BBD song – you know, Bell Biv Devoe? The guys from New Edition?"

"Never heard of them," she deadpanned, "but I am also confused about your motives. What were your motives or intentions with Jon and Robert?"

"I toyed with the idea of dating Jon that night and making him my man, but all I knew for sure that night was that Robert had my attention because of how much he reminded me of Jesus. I drove home wondering if Robert or Jon would call me first and it was Robert. It was almost 4 am. I was knocked out, my black out shades were drawn and my eye-mask was over my eyes as usual; working at 112, I needed to sleep during daylight 3 times a week. I am surprised I even answered the phone after all the drinking, dancing and cavorting around town – I didn't even wrap my hair up! What I didn't know, was that Jazz had given him the address and phone number and he was outside my apartment at a payphone when he called!"

"Were you upset that she had done that?" inquired Dr. Williams.

"No, even though I was genuinely surprised he was there, I wanted to be with him anyway. So, I let him in, although I played like I didn't know what was going on at first."

"So what happened?" She asked, so I started to tell her what happened from when I answered the phone until breakfast that next afternoon, but little did I know – Lil' Miss Prissy had some words for me too.

"When I answered the phone all I heard was, "Janine. Janine, wake up baby. It's Robert. What's your bell honey? I am outside, I know you're not asleep already girl," he said with a smile in his voice. I was shocked but pleased; I'd fell asleep with my hands between my legs, imagining his mouth on my pearl and his fingers inside me.

"Hey Rob, what are you doing here? Mishie gave you my address too?" I laughed. "My bell is 104 and I live in apartment 10 on the 4th floor… What are you doing he…"?

"You know what I am here for girl," he cut me off abruptly. "I am here for the same reason you gave me your number. Couldn't go home with you on my mind…had to come taste that. I will be right up."

I paused the story to let her know what I was doing after he abruptly hung up. "When he hung up as if he just knew he was getting in, I cut the phone ringer off, lit my candles and quickly rinsed my mouth out with some mouthwash." Dr Williams looked as if she was on the verge of saying something I didn't want to hear; she pushed her black and white, Fendi glasses up on her nose, looked me in the eyes with a surprisingly stern expression for such a young lady, so I quickly asked – "What was I supposed to do?"

"What do you mean 'supposed' to do? I cannot tell you what you should have or should not have done. I am here to help you understand how you got to this point in your marriage and sex life and what or if you want to change. However, I do have a question for you. Where were your boundaries?"

"Boundaries? What do boundaries have to do with anything?" I asked sarcastically. But thought to myself, she was saying I let people get too close too soon, but physical closeness was what I wanted. It was much easier when there was no real mental or emotional connection involved, to let them go. So I amended, "Actually, I do know what you mean Dr. Williams, but boundaries were unimportant at the time, I had a physical urge, a need that needed to be fulfilled, as well as an emotional one. I hadn't been held in a long time."

"You do realize that there are people who go for long stretches of time, even years, without having sexual contact with anyone, not even themselves. I just want you to think about that and while we are apart this week think about why that may be beneficial." She paused and looked at me for a momentarily contemplating something then continued, "Before we part, I want to recap what I am hearing about why you are here and what we are going to work on during our visits. You have had an encounter with sexual molestation, had your heart broken in your first long-term relationship with a young man and these things have left you feeling in some ways that men and even your own family cannot be trusted with your emotional and physical welfare. You expressed a brief same sex relationship in your early adolescence that you found to be enjoyable, but have not discussed pursuing since. You enjoy sex immensely to the point of engaging in the act with men whom you don't know fully, in order to be gratified sexually. You also realize from our discussion that you have not taken into consideration the men in your life when making decisions regarding your sexuality and now you would like to change this pattern of behaviors as it relates to your husband. Am I correct in my assessment of the current situation?"

When she said all of that in one mouthful, I felt 3 feet tall. She was completely and totally correct in what she said but "*Damn! Was that me?*" I sat there dumbfounded unable to comment for a minute then uttered, "When you just said all that about me just now, I initially thought that you were speaking of some other woman. It didn't sound like the person I envision when I think about who I am, but it is. I sat in my car before I came in here looking at myself wondering if I needed to be here, thinking I look like a youthful, successful, married woman, but I recognize that I am so much more under the surface of that facade that is cracked, shattered and needs help to heal."

Dr. Williams looked at her watch and gently said to me, "Well, our time is up for today, but I am glad that you have decided to make the change. The first step is admitting your part in your troubles and the second is the commitment to making a change. Do you feel like this is a change that you can commit to?"

I paused for a moment to consider what had just happened, *"Am I really ready to change how I see sex and relationships? Do I really think my husband will forgive me?"* I questioned myself, silently realizing that all I have are questions. I knew I had to at least make a sincere effort, let the chips fall where they may. I finally replied, "Yes, Dr. Williams, I believe this is change that I can commit to. I also want to thank you for allowing me to speak freely. I look forward to our meeting next week."

"Well, Mrs. Dupont, I look forward to our next meeting as well," replied Dr. Williams. Make sure you think about your commitment to this change when faced with decisions that might jeopardize what you hold dear. See you next week," she added.

CHAPTER 5
Robert: Forbidden Fruit

Here I am sitting in my office – head in hands, wondering how all of this came crashing down around me. I thought I had finally gotten the upper hand in this whole scenario, but it still seems like I am the one shafted in the end. I wanted Janine then and I still do. I remember the first time I had her; I had to show off - give her the raw uncut, all so she'd be open on me and forget about Jon.

That morning after we all hung out, I showed up at Janine's house tryna figure out how I was gonna get in, I mean, her girl gave me the address, but only with a little finagling from me. I convinced her that Janine wanted me to have it, it was easy; she was tipsy. I played it real pimp on the phone with her, making it seem like she knew what I know she did, but didn't want to seem like a slut. I figured the less conversation the better. "Just let me in," I was thinking, "I can show you why you should, better than I can tell you."

Janine came to the door all champagne and Chanel. For a moment, I was stuck staring at her sheer white tee; nipples lookin' me in the face begging me to kiss them - I was instantly at attention. I grabbed her by the nape of her neck and the small of her back and stuck my tongue down her throat, she wrapped her tight little body around mine like a glove and sparring tongues battled by her door for what felt like an infinity. I slowed the tempo, pulling back and nibbling on her lips and gently kneading her right breast. Then, I pinched her right nipple and kissed it through the sheerness of her shirt. She was panting as I put my hand inside her panties from behind and slid my finger into her wet crevice to find that button, I pressed it and she gasped and pulled away from me breathlessly saying, "Damn." Then took my hand and led me through her apartment to her bedroom door. When we got there, she stopped and said, "Do you have protection?"

I replied, "Magnums, babygirl."

She looked at me with a slight smile that said she had heard that before and said, "Good. Take off your shoes. Whatever goes down in here has to stay here. If you tell anyone Robert, all bets are off and you will never be allowed back into my boudoir. I don't do campus guys. You're my first."

She was at my chest looking up at me and I could smell the fresh mint on her tongue I'd just tasted and I wondered if she brushed her teeth before she opened the door. I smiled, glad she wanted to impress me, but I wanted to see just how much and how hard she would OG for me. I took off my shoes, but didn't reply; I just reached past her to the doorknob and swung open the door. There was no one I could tell about my coming here, but I didn't need to talk about my conquests; I left that up to Jon.

That room was made for all night sex, black floor-length drapes that made it seem like midnight even though it was daybreak, my feet sank into some kind of fur on her floor and the queen-sized bed was raised; exposing black satin sheets with a velvet comforter at the foot. Smelling of honey, bourbon and vanilla, mixed with her scent, the candles she lit that gave the room the perfect glow and ambiance with Chante Moore singing softly in the background. I was impressed and that is hard to do, but honey had me here behind my best friend's back, so impressed was a gross understatement; I was compelled. The entire time she was winding on Jon at the party, Janine's eyes bored holes into me; when she closed her eyes, I knew she was fantasizing about me being inside her. I knew Jon was rock hard by the way he gyrated against her apple bottom, but by the way she moved and watched me, I knew she was wet and thinking of me. I had a feeling Jon was gonna mess it up and not take his chance; he thought he wanted a "good girl." I was dancing with her girl, Jazzy, who I knew had a man 'cause I tried to talk to her last year and of course she reminded me, but was looking over her head at Janine, nodding my head the entire time - encouraging her to give it to him.

I looked down at her and said, "Take all that off Janine, I want to see you." She obliged wordlessly and let me take her all in; perky petite breasts with taut almost burgundy nipples, small, nipped-in waist and flat tummy that drew my eyes to the small strip of closely cropped hair covering her mound. Her clit was swollen already, I could see it peeking out, winking at me. Instead of taking off my clothes in return, I turned her around, bent her over, dropped to my knees and buried my face in that sweet ass.

She moaned deep and low in her throat as I spread her cheeks and let my tongue roam her slit from behind, she touched her toes and I grabbed her clit with my lips suckling what I could reach of it, lightly using my tongue to flick what I couldn't reach with lips, making her gasp and stutter, "Ra-Ra-Ra-Robert, please…".

"Please what baby?" I stopped my sweet assault and asked tenderly.

"Don't stop," she said breathlessly.

I chuckled and her knees buckled as I let her go to stand up, so I caught her and laid her on the bed. She looked at me glassy eyed and said, "Take off your clothes Robert, I want to taste you back."

I said, "Nah... Babygirl, this is all you, let me do the pleasing, just lay back." I was tired of chicks on campus trying to throw their panties at me; offering to give me blowjobs at the drop of a dime, I wanted to please and this was my chance. I undressed slowly for her, knowing my shoulder tribal tats were impressive with my biceps rippling. My abs were washboard hard and as I stripped my boxers off and stood erect, I saw her eyes widen.

She started stammering, "Robert, I..."

"Don't worry baby, you'll be ready when it's time for me to put it down."

"Okay... but I, Robert - I never... had... anyone so..."

"Shhhhh... I got you babygirl, I'm not gonna knock the bottom out. Don't worry, trust me."

I settled down between her legs, placed my hand on either thigh and looked at her; I wanted to take her all in before I began to lay in on her. I breathed my breath hot on her opening, making her shiver and squirm, ran my tongue from stem to stern, then kissed her lips, sticking my tongue into her hole, tasting her creamy nectar. After a while of my ministrations, she started to mewl deep in her throat, so I paused my licking and stuck my finger inside her and her hips began to buck against my hand. I caught her rhythm making sure the heel of my hand was right against her clit and placed my other hand just under her belly button applying firm pressure.

Janine wet the bed under her, her juices flowing while she rotated her pelvis against my hand. I slid in another finger to make sure she was ready and Janine moaned aloud, "Ahhh," and said loudly, "Oh my *God!* Robert, *please!*"

"Please what? You think your ready baby? Tell me... tell me you're ready baby," I begged her.

"Yes baby. Yes. Please. Now. Baby..."

I felt like I would bust, but I knew it was gonna be a long morning for us both. I put the magnum on as she watched, waiting for me to put it in. I eased down over her, nudged her knees wide and held them up under my arms while I entered her. Her legs began to quiver, then shake, but I didn't want her to move before I felt that spot. She was so tight and slippery; I wanted to take the rubber off just so I could feel her wetness. She came faster, and faster; squeezing me tighter and tighter with every wave, it was too good to be true. I finally got all the way inside her and rested on her G-spot flexing my muscles so that my tip tapped her spot and she just mewled, "Eaah, eaah, eaah", with each pulse.

I let her legs go and she wrapped them around my waist tightly, so I leaned in close and ground my hips to make sure I hit every spot, then I took her mouth roughly shoving my tongue in as I started to buck on her, making her take it all for a few rapid strokes.

Janine yelped, "I can't take it! Ahhh! Ahh! Ahh! I can't take it! Damn! Robert damn! Ahhh! Ahhh!"

She kept trying to get away even though her legs were shaking uncontrollably and I could feel her wetness damn near squirting with every down stroke. She never had a man hit the bottom like that, I knew at that moment, she was mine and it was going to be on with us for the long haul.

We made love all morning, well into the afternoon; I could not believe her stamina, especially after being up damn near all night. We talked between sessions and I found out that she was a night owl because she worked at Club 112 overnight, three days a week. I also found out that babygirl had been without a man for about three months, so she was ripe.

She made me a down home Sunday breakfast like she was from the dirty-dirty: grits, eggs over easy, bacon, scrapple, toast, fried apples and home-fries all from scratch, all like my grandma makes before church, even fresh squeezed orange juice! I was surprised because at first glance, she seemed like all the other spoiled New York girls that populate Spelman's campus, but her demeanor and style of dress hid the traditional values she seemed to have at that moment – she was a contradiction, which made her even more attractive to me.

After she made our plates and joined me at the kitchen island to eat, she said, "You know what? I must really be feeling you or maybe it's the way you just put it down in there!" she said, her head nodding toward the bedroom. "I never cook for any of my boyfriends, I make them take me out all the time. Gotta make 'em think I can't cook 'cause I don't need them asking me to cook all the time!" She laughed out loud for a minute at her lies. "Plus, I don't want them getting ideas, I didn't want to be any of their wives," she said looking at me seriously.

Over breakfast Janine told me so much about herself… I was surprised until she told me that I reminded her of her very first boyfriend. That niggah broke her heart though and I wanted her to be my princess; she was hood enough to fit in with my crazy, country ass family and bourgeoisie enough for me to take with me to the NFL. Karen's spot was just about taken after one night with honey!

Janine kept reminding me of my mother; all tough on the outside but really easy going and soft, once you broke past the tough exterior. She wanted a man but didn't need one she could outthink or who couldn't make her submit to his will without force. She was a beautiful and resilient, yet vulnerable young woman and I wanted to be that strong man for her.

I realized after she shared her story that it was the typical pretty chick story; absentee father and a string of "uncles" who dated her mother, but paid her no mind except for one, who could never really replace that father figure in her life. There were so many beautiful women out there without that emotional strength and that made them easy prey. However, after being with her and talking to her that afternoon, I wanted to make her love me how she loved her first boyfriend; I never thought I would cause her the same kind of pain he did. Janine and I were inseparable for about four months, but because I was still involved with Karen, my high school girlfriend and I'd failed to end it right, everything came crumbling down around me.

I was a player in every sense of the word back then. It was too easy to have sex with multiple women without any of them knowing or if they did know; they accepted it because I was NFL bound and had all the Benjamins. It was really hard for me to accept that she left me cold and took Karen with her. Karen knew what I was about and what I was doing on the side the whole time, but with Janine, it was different; I stopped fuckin' around literally and figuratively, but I held onto Karen; she was my high school girlfriend, who lived in my old neighborhood. I even toyed with the idea of marrying her when I got to the NFL, but Janine messed that up for her. Then Karen came up to my off campus apartment one day, while I wasn't there and Janine was!

From what my next-door neighbor said, Karen knocked on the door and Janine answered it. They didn't get the entire conversation, but they said they heard Karen say, "Who the hell are you and why the hell are you in my man's house?" and Janine replied, "I'm his woman, which is why I am in here when he's not. Plus, I have keys to come and go as I please. Do you?" My neighbor said Karen didn't reply at first, but then she said, "You know what, I don't have keys and honestly miss, I ain't even got a squabble with you. I just think I deserve a little truth after spending six years of my life with a man who obviously can't tell it. Maybe you will."

My neighbor said that after Karen said that, Neene let her in and he didn't hear any noise. He was obviously watching to see if they started fighting or if the police were called because he said after a little while, Karen just left the house and a short while after that so did Neene. The difference was that Neene was crying and carrying an overnight bag and Karen just looked pissed as hell.

Karen came to me that next week after I called her and Janine like a stalker day and night to find out what happened between them. She just came and knocked on the door that day, and when I let her in, she stood right inside the foyer and said real slowly in her sweet southern drawl, "Robert, I never thought there could be another girl out here that could replace me in your heart. Your bed – I wasn't sweating because I know that you are young and we weren't married or engaged yet, but your heart – you said it would be mine forever."

"I know... I messed up Karen."

"No, you knew what you were doing Robert. You wanted her real bad and you wanted her to replace me. But now that I told her everything, she ain't gonna go with you no more and you know what?"

"What?"

"Neither am I. I am a fine woman Robert. I can be with any man I want. I chose you, but you went and chose her – it might have worked out if you had 'a gotten around to telling me it was over, but you tried to string me along just in case your "*New York City Girlfriend*" didn't work out. Hmph - jokes on you Jack," she said, then turned opened the door back up and cold walked right out of my life taking the love of my life with her.

CHAPTER 6
Jon: Meeting of Minds

Here I am walking into the waiting room of Douglas Detective Agency and I can't believe I am about to tell one of my oldest friends that I think my wife is cheating on me. Even though we haven't been all that close over the past eighteen years, it still makes me feel uncomfortable; I mean, he knows both of us and was there at the beginning... That's why he's the perfect man for the job.

As soon as I walked in I noticed there were cameras peering at me from several angles. The look and feel of his office was all high-tech chrome with white leather furniture and glass accents. It was shiny and distracting, yet calming. I guess that's what people need when they come here to find out things they don't really want to know – distracting, yet calming.

I wonder if Robert looked the same; he had all that hair in college – Is he balding? That would be funny – I mean not funny, but come on son! That full head of curls was one thing he banked on to get the girls! I doubt he's even in field condition – It's been years since he was on the football field.

"Good Morning Mr. Dupont, Mr. Matthews will be with you in a few minutes. Please have a seat. Can I get you some coffee? Tea? A croissant or muffin?"

"No, thank you." I was too nervous to drink or eat a thing.

"You can call me Agnes."

"No thank you, Ms. Agnes."

Mrs. Agnes Washington chuckled, "That's okay as well Mr. Dupont. If you want anything, please let me know."

I just smiled in response, I was wildly surprised that his secretary looked like someone's grandmother: all grey curly hair and cat-eyed spectacles. He was such a lady-killer in college and the NFL; guess I was expecting a model, not a nana. I wanted to ask her for one of those freshly baked croissants and cup of that heavenly smelling Ecuadorian roast, but it was too much to take in at once; I thought my stomach might rebel and I would either throw up all over my crispy white linen suit or have the bubble guts, so I just sat tight and waited. I was ten minutes early, but I guess he was going to have me wait until my actual appointment time to see me, which sucked. I mean we went way back right? I really came early because I wanted to check out the office and make sure it wasn't some seedy spot. I was astounded at the spanking new development it was in - I hadn't even gotten a bid in on this one. I usually got in on all the building bids in the Greater Atlanta area, but this one went under my radar for some reason.

"Mr. Matthews will see you now," Nana Agnes interrupted my thought.

"Thank you Ms. Agnes," I said smiling. She reminded me of my Aunt Kizzie: feisty and kind, all at the same time.

I walked through the mahogany door, impressed with the weight of it and apprehensive of what was getting ready to go down.

"Come on in Jon my man! Sorry to keep you waiting like that, I was on a conference call. Did you get one of those muffins out there or some coffee?"

He was way too happy to see me there I thought instinctively, but I went with it and replied, "Nah man! I am not trying to go too far past the 190 lb. mark on the scale. We ain't young buck athletes no more!" Then, he stood up and I saw that perhaps I was the only one who wasn't still an athlete; Robert was a solid mass of muscle. He was wearing an impeccably cut navy Armani suit with a pale pink shirt and diamond earrings in both ears that belied his manhood. Rob walked around his massive mahogany desk to shake my hand and I must admit, I was a little resentful of his ability to stay in shape after all these years. My desk job and all the travel I did for business didn't leave much time for my old workout routine; I was all soft in the middle and my small pot belly hanging over my Gucci linen embarrassed me.

He shook my hand more firmly than I liked and said, "So, Jon. What brings you here?"

"I am beginning to think that my life isn't what I think," I replied.

"Humph. What do you mean Jon? I have been doing this kind of thing, security and P.I. work, for about five years now and from what I know of you and Janine, your relationship doesn't fit the specs."

"Specs? What specs?"

"The wife who isn't cared for emotionally or physically by her husband is the one that usually tends to stray and the husband usually knows why his wife is going out on him, but doesn't want to admit it's his fault. Those are the specs. From what I remember of your relationship, you two were thick as thieves and were eye to eye with one another on every level. Shoot, that's why I never got married – couldn't find that with anyone else, I was even a little jealous."

"Jealous! You have got to be kidding me! You were the NFL super star. I never even made the NBA draft."

"Nigga please! All that fame and money I made didn't make me happy. I could never find my own woman to help me stay on the straight and narrow, have my back – ya' know? Every chick I dated, dated me for the money. I messed up on my down home first love – Karen. Remember her?"

"Yeah man! She was the beautiful chocolate girl with the long black hair and the big down home, corn fed…"

"Yeah! Yeah! Yeah! Man. Come on man! Don't talk about Karen like that man, damn!" He laughed, then quickly sobered, "Seriously though Jon, in the midst of losing her, I lost the only other woman I thought could be the "one", so I missed my chance at love. You found her – or at least I thought you did."

"So did I Rob, so did I. I think I remember when you and Karen broke up; wasn't it right around the time me and Janine hooked up? She'd called me looking for you and I told her I hadn't seen you, but you might be home. I had *"fine Leslie"* with me, that's how I remember – you 'member Leslie with the real big titties right?" Robert just looked at me with a strange expression on his face, but I continued. I figured he was just trying to remember what happened.

"Well, I remember because I was in the middle of getting some brains from Leslie when the phone just kept ringing and ringing like someone was calling and hanging up and then calling right back. Leslie made me answer it! She was all like, 'That phone is breaking my concentration Jon, just answer it already! Damn', so I did, and it was Karen saying she had been calling you, but not getting an answer for like over two or three weeks and was worried. She was all apologizing for calling – I couldn't even be mad at her, she sounded real upset. I just told her to go to the house to get her off the phone."

"You did, huh?"

"Yeah... Why did y'all break up Robert?"

"She caught me with my new shorty and they both left me." Robert replied, stone faced.

"*Damn*! I didn't know you had a new shorty back then. That's why your ass was MIA huh? I know you didn't even let random shorties come to your crib. You know you was on some secret squirrel shit with the ladies. She must have been a bad joint for you to... Damn, that's f'd up though man." I chuckled and shook my head at the same time. I had no idea that this cat had someone he was in love with leave him, much less two chicks. No wonder his love life was such a public mess when he was in the NFL!

"Jon, why are you here? What can I do, for you?" Robert said abruptly.

"I want you to trail Janine, man. I think she's cheating on me."

CHAPTER 7
Robert: Seeing Red

My mind screamed - *What in the hell just happened?* And instantly began to ache as Jon closed the door to my office. After I watched him make small talk with my Aunt Agnes on the closed circuit camera and leave, I hit the intercom.

"Agnes, cancel all of my appointments for the rest of the day. I am headed out."

"What's wrong nephew?"

"Nothin'. I just need to take a break after that last one."

"I thought Jon was your old friend from Morehouse honey…"

"I don't want to talk about it." I said cutting her off sharply.

"Well, fine then," she said sounding more hurt than offended. She was the only one in my family that stood by me when I got that drug charge and was put off the team. It was crazy, all the family I helped buy homes and gave thousands of my hard-earned money to, would

63

not accept my calls from prison. It was eye opening and heart wrenching at the same time.

I sat at my desk stewing, then re-thought my decision not to talk to Auntie. Who else was there to talk to anyway?

I hit the intercom and said cheerfully, "Aunt Aggie, you wanna come wit' me ta' get something ta' eat?

"Are you sure you want my company?" She asked, still sounding a little hurt.

"'Course – You're my favorite auntie, Auntie Aggie!"

She chuckled, "Yeah, okay Bobby big-head. I am your only Auntie! But, I 'cept your apology. Where are we goin' ta' eat?"

"Good, I was getting worried…" I laughed. "Wherever you want is fine with me."

"I want to go to Chantelle's. They are the only ones who make that peach cobbler like your momma used to. I been missing little sis something terrible lately…"

"Mommy… Wow! Her peach cobbler was better than Big Mamma's! You and her, man y'all were all I had. God better be taking better care of my momma's heart than I did." I shook my head dejected. She died of a heart attack shortly after I was arrested. I still carry the weight of her death with me daily. Being at her funeral in chains was the most embarrassing and dishonorable moment in my life. I never knew my dad, but I never missed him with Big Daddy and my five uncles to help guide me into manhood. My momma was my heart and her older sister was like my second mother.

"Let's go Auntie," I said walking out of my office with my suit jacket in hand.

We arrived at Chantelle's' and immediately my mouth started to water! That roasted rosemary chicken smelled like heaven! It almost made me forget my troubles. We sat at Auntie's favorite spot by the window and before I could sit down after pulling out her chair, she went in on me.

"Bobby baby, what is going on? What did that young man say that upset you so?"

"Auntie he brought up something that happened a long time ago… Made me think about what my life could have been."

"Come on baby, we all know that God doesn't make mistakes. It may hurt somethin' terrible at first, but the lesson is always there if you look at it right."

"I know Auntie but this lesson never showed up. Only the heartache and pain." I said quietly.

"So, it's about that girl."

"What girl auntie?"

"That *New York City* girl from college."

"You remember her Auntie!" I said.

"Of course, chile; Auntie never seen you look at a girl like that before, nor since. We all thought for sure you were gonna marry that big booty Karen with the long hair – Shoot! She'd been around since damn near pre-school. Your uncles even bet their money on her, but I bet my money on that other one. But she's been around ever since though, I thought. What was her name again? Janie?" she said absentmindedly.

"That is what I used to call her from this book I read in high school."

"Yah sir! I know that book baby – so you musta been Tea Cake then huh honey! Ha!" She laughed but quickly sobered up, remembering I was hurtin'.

"You don't get it Auntie." I said miserably, and then I looked up and saw the waitress standing there waiting.

"Afternoon Mr. Matthews. What can I get you both today?" She said all cheery, making me wanna cuss in her smiling face.

"I want the regular. You, auntie?"

"I want my regular too honey, but I want some ice cream with my cobbler today."

"You got it – Aunt Agatha." she said then sauntered off.

65

"Well... baby... Don't ever think ya have the market cornered on heartache and pain. Now, Aunt Agatha has had her fair share of sorrow! My first and what I thought would be my only real love was this man named Joseph. Now this here man was fine, Bobbie, I mean wavy hair, light brown, strong and tall," she said shaking her head slightly, looking out the window at her past. "He was the only man I ever loved real deep, but he was taken from me. It took me a long time to love your uncle Kenneth and even with all of his courting and loving up on me, it took me a long time to really even allow myself to feel anything for him."

"How was Joseph taken from you Auntie? Did he die?"

"Yes chile," she whispered – "He died in 'Nam. Just left one day and never came back home again."

"Wow Auntie... I am so sorry..."

"Don't be sorry for me." She said cutting him off. "Baby, I had a love that many people don't get ta' experience, so I am and was blessed. The thing is... I was blessed twice – got ta' love hard more than once. But letting go of that first real love was hard to do..." she paused then added – "Spill it Bobbie baby. What did your friend have to do with you losing Janie?"

"Jon has her." I said simply.

Auntie just shook her head sadly and said, "Well honey, just how close are you and this Jon fella anyway? Do you have to work for him on his case? Matter 'a fact, I don't remember him at any of the court dates and I remember her at a few of them, I could have sworn..."

When she said that, a flood of memories came back about how Jon and I grew apart and it all started over some pussy. I never talked about my women, but Jon *had* to tell everyone who he was dealing with – it was an annoying and bitch-assed trait of his I hated. The stories were amusing at first but a week or so before we met Janine at Club 112, I found out that he was sexin' one

66

of my exes! What's crazy is not only that he told me, but how.

We were sitting in the cafe, it was mad hot outside and he had just come in. Me and Marcus were sitting there, eating burgers and fries and just chillin', when he just bust out with this story – "Son. I just had the best head this side of the Mason Dixon line! On my word, that bitch had the deep throat of LIFE! I didn't think those sorority chicks got down like that but that butterscotch, freckled-face freak let me stick my dick in every orifice on her body! I thought she was gonna let me do it to her in her ear hole!" Then, he just bust out laughing. I just looked at him with my mouth open at first, and then I quickly closed it and got up. Marcus was chuckling until he noticed my face, then I could see that he realized what I had – that he was talking about Leslie, the same chick I had been sleeping with on the side for six months. Jon's self-serving, oblivious ass never even noticed the exchange or my getting up. I guess he just thought I was done, which I was. From that moment on, it was war and once we met Janine, she was gonna be mine, no matter what.

CHAPTER 8
Janine: Revelations

I left Dr. Tasha's office that day thinking about a church service a few months ago when Bishop taught on the book of Hosea. God told Hosea, a priest, to marry Gomer who was known to be a loose woman. Hosea didn't want to, but ever faithful, he did what he was told and married Gomer. He not only married Gomer, but he loved her. He loved her so much that he forgot who she was before they were married and so did she or seemed to at first, but eventually, Gomer returned to her ways; sleeping with someone else and not returning home for days on end. She even told Hosea brazenly that she was cheating on him. It got to the point where Hosea had no idea if the three children he took care of in her long absences were even his.

    Bishop talked about how God commanded Hosea not only to love Gomer again, but He then told Hosea to go find her and save her from being sold into slavery by one of her so called friends. He also told Hosea that someone else was in love with her. So not only did Hosea have to forgive her for all of her transgressions, a necessity to be able to love someone after being betrayed, but he also had to go looking for Gomer, and pay to get back his wife, who by the way, was loved by someone else.

To me it seemed like God was tripping! I mean, wasn't Hosea the one that was wronged in this situation? That Gomer was crazy – I mean she had a husband that loved her and a family that was respected in the community - Why would she sacrifice all of that... Suddenly, it all began to make sense. I began to feel a wave of conviction as I sat behind my husband, the deacon, in the second pew. My eyes darted back and forth under the wide brim of my pale yellow hat and I leaned forward and my upper lip began to sweat. Then, sinking back against the soft cushion in my pew, I cautiously glanced around at my fellow worshippers at Christ's Living Well Baptist Ministries. 'Did Sister Lodell just look at me and shake her head? Wait! Did Sister Jolene Adams cut her eyes my way? They knew?' I closed my eyes tried to center myself by taking a deep breath, quickly exhaled and thought 'No the spirit just wants me to hear this.' But, I didn't want to - I felt overwhelmed and exposed, so I decided to flee to the only place in the church there were no speakers – the restroom.

I tapped Jon and he turned and smiled slightly, I returned the smile, leaned over and said "Going to take Amber to the bathroom, be right back." There was no better excuse than to take mama's little pumkin' to the ladies room.

She looked up at me and whispered, "But I don't have to go potty mommy."

I just muttered absent mindedly, "Shush, Amber, it's okay, just come with mommy 'kay?" I grabbed her hand and lead her down the side aisle reciting a litany to myself, 'No one knows, No one knows, No one knows.'

In retrospect, my getting up and leaving the sanctuary during Bishop's "Hosea" sermon may have been an admission of some kind of guilt and I probably should have stayed my behind in my seat! I knew for sure that Jon didn't know all of my transgressions at that time, but I did. I knew I had been cheating on him in my heart and intentions from the very beginning of our relationship by loving Robert and although for a while I was a good wife, loneliness lured me back to Robert, but because he began to push me to leave my husband, I knew it was time to cut him off. It wasn't just the lonely though, it seemed like there was a space being adored by a man even for just a short while filled, even if it was just for that moment that they were inside me. I felt like a real woman when a man showed his affection for me in any way; sexually, flirting, just a look on the street from a random man made my day. I felt hollow thinking about it; was Jon's love not enough for me? Was I Gomer? It made me wonder why the Bible doesn't tell us why Gomer behaved in that way.

I was glad I made Amber go to the restroom with me because, despite her protests; mama's pumpkin really did have to go. We made it back to the sanctuary just in time for Bishop to explain how this relates to our faith. In Hosea's letter to Israel in the Bible, he likened his situation with Gomer to how God loved Israel despite her constant infidelity towards His laws. If God could take Israel back, sacrifice His only son and then love her like she never betrayed Him by forgiving her, then I just pray that Jon will be able to do the same for me.

My cell phone disturbed my reverie, that sermon really stuck with me! It was Robert – damn! Should I answer it? I blew him off today without so much as a call, to get my mind together for my therapy appointment. Jon somehow scheduled my appointment at the same time and day I usually meet with Robert, which seemed a little suspicious to me. Wednesday was also the same day Jon Jr. had his car crash, which was not too far from my rendezvous location at the Prime Town Center W Hotel too. I don't believe in consequences, so I am gonna have to end this with Robert today before it all blows up in my face.

"Hey babe, what's up?" I said nonchalantly.

"You tell me, I called you earlier 'cause you didn't meet me like you said..." he started, salty.

"I know honey," I did not need an irate man with a license to carry on my hands! "I had an appointment that just came up unexpectedly..."

"You could have called me though, come on Janie you know..."

"I know Robert, but I do want to see you. Can we meet now?"

"Lemme call you back baby, I have a client coming in, so give me a half, 'kay?"

"Okay, I'll meet you in Tabu. I'm starving and their mushroom pot-stickers are calling me. See you in a little while."

****

I walked into Tabu and was instantly relaxed. The candlelit tables were shimmering with flickering light as I pushed past the curtains and the throng in the Living Room. It instantly put my mind at ease. My husband hated Japanese food, so I never ran the risk of seeing him here or running into any of his friends. He was the leader of that pack without Robert in the mix, so whatever Jon said, they did; whatever he didn't like, neither did they. I loved Japanese food, sushi especially. Shoot! I even loved Japanese inspired fashion – he didn't know it, but those heels he loved to see me naked in were Hara-Juku Lovers and completely Japanese inspired! I chuckled to myself as I was seated at a table for two by a beautiful young woman with piercing green eyes.

"Would you like your usual Miss?" she asked quietly.

"Yes, thank you Kim, but give me a glass of Riesling today, I'm having a hell of a day so far and its only 1:00."

"As you please, I'll be right back with your glass of wine."

As she walked away, I noticed how she was slight as a reed; slender and pliable, her waist length, jet-black hair tied away from her face simply enhanced her elegance her simple beauty calmed my nerves for a moment. I was so hungry and yet so preoccupied with the day's events and implications, I drank all of my wine before my light lunch appeared and when I looked up after eating only a bite of a mushroom pot-sticker, Robert was standing in front of me.

"Hey you," he said softly.

"Hey babe," I replied, looking at him thinking, 'Damn! Either the wine has me trippin' or he is looking extra good to me right now... Probably because I know it's over.'

"Let's go upstairs, I want to..."

"Let me finish eating please baby," I interrupted and stuffed the rest of the pot-sticker into my mouth, greedily talking with my mouth full. "I haven't eaten all day. That appointment earlier stole my appetite and I have been craving these since I left her office."

"Okay love, let me order something too then. Are you taking the day today? I don't want you to go out of your routine, but I have some things I need to get off..." he said suggestively.

I grinned as I instantly felt myself swell and moisten. I looked at him and put another pot-sticker to my mouth letting my tongue lightly lick it before I bit into it. Robert smiled at me and I was struck at his beauty; caramel brown eyes, full top lip and pearlescent white teeth – he was an amalgamation of all the physical qualities a perfect man could possess. He reached across the table; his long fingers hand grabbed my petite ones and brought the rest of the pot-sticker to his mouth.

"That's good," he said softly as he held my hand from across the table.

Kim appeared quietly with another glass of Riesling for me, and Robert ordered the duck spring rolls and a small bottle of San Pellegrino.

"So, I guess you are not going back to work today huh?" he said pointedly, looking at my glass of wine.

"No. I took the day. There have been some interesting developments in my life as of late and I need this time to think especially after that appointment."

"What was this appointment you keep talking about?"

"I had to see a therapist today."

"Had to? What? What do you mean you had to Janie?"

I smiled at his nickname for me thinking, if only he could be my Teacake in reality, then said, "I think Jon knows about us. I am pretty sure he knows I'm cheating on him. I don't understand why you had to give blood at the hospital Robert. "

Robert looked shocked then said, "So why the therapist? I would have thought that he'd just ask for a divorce. Isn't that what you want anyway; to be free, to be mine?" his thick eyebrows knitted in confusion.

"He doesn't want to end our marriage without fighting for it. He is the never say die type who can't admit he's made a mistake." I said, derision filling my voice. What I didn't say was that I loved my husband so much for not giving up on me and our family. I paused and added, "He thinks I have a problem so the therapist is to fix me and bring me back to him as the woman he thought I was, so we can continue living our lives out as he planned them. If I don't go, he's going to take the kids Robert. I can't let that happen."

Robert ran his hands through his dark curls and shook his head. I could tell his mind was spinning with what I said insinuated, but there was more I just couldn't bear to say. Suddenly, all I wanted was to feel his weight on top of me and feel his tongue in my mouth as he drilled his strength into me – that would make all of this go away, if only for a little while. Kim arrived noiselessly with Robert's spring rolls and I asked for the check.

Robert glanced up at me, "I love you, Janie. I always have, and I am willing to fight for you and the kids."

I hid my shock at his admission but it rocked me. "Okay," I said to myself. *'I will just give him some this last time to make us both feel better, then I will break it to him – I want my family, I love my husband and I have to make our relationship work for the sake of my children.'* I didn't respond, instead I said to him slowly, "Eat your food babe. You are going to need ALL your strength this afternoon."

I looked on as he wolfed down his spring rolls, slightly amused, but also bewildered at my own behavior. I was supposed to be turning over a new leaf; instead I was sitting here salivating, my va-j-j thumping in anticipation of this man bending me over. Didn't I say I wanted to be a better wife? Be the woman my husband deserved? Damn! Robert's pecs were distracting me – pulsating every time he lifted his hand to his mouth. I do want to be that woman, but what about Robert? Even if after I say this today, he will still be here in my heart.

Before I could dwell on that, Kim sidled up to me with the check, I looked at her absentmindedly and Robert said, "Here Kim, put it on my Black Card." His attempt to sound important seemed foolish, but was genuine. I sometimes forget Robert is the owner/lead Detective of the Douglass Detective Agency. He just seems like the same old 'football player from college Robert' he has always been to me.

Kim brought his card back; I stood as he finished signing it and said, "Lead the way lover."

He grinned, "Now, that's what I'm talking about," he grabbed his briefcase, took my hand and led me back through the crowd of people in the Living Room to the elevators. When the doors closed, he pulled me to him and held me saying, " I know it's been a rough few weeks love, and I saw the story about JD on the news. Let me take you away from all that for a little while - Okay?"

What could I say to that? He was the sweetest lover I'd ever known, always took his time with me and listened to my feelings. I don't know if it was the wine or my feeling overwhelmed, but I began to sob softly into his shoulder. We stepped off of the mirrored elevator into the hall on the 12th floor and he let me get out my sorrows on his shoulder until it was damp from my eyes and runny nose. When my sobbing subsided, he lifted my chin, wiped my eyes and nose with his sleeve, briefly peered into my eyes, grabbed my hand and led me down the hall to our suite. In suite 112, the bed was turned down just how we liked it with candles lit, and shades drawn; making the broad light of day dissipate into a romantic scene ready to make my dreary troubles disappear. I stood in the middle of the suite, eyes closed thinking about the last few hours, felt Robert's hands cup my face gently and his full mouth kiss my eyelids softly.

"Let me undress you love," he murmured.

"'Kay." I whispered.

He lifted my calf, kissed my ankle and removed my 4-inch heels deftly. As I stood flat-footed in front of him, he slid his hands up my skirt to the top of my garter and released my thigh-high stockings and while he tugged them down my thighs, Robert buried his face in my crotch warming my center. After sliding the stockings over my feet one at a time, he reached up to unzip my skirt letting it fall into a pool of satin around my feet. Robert worked his way up my body, palming then kneading my behind, and then he stood and unbuttoned my blouse, cuffs and front, quickly disrobing me. I stood in front of him in my black lace feeling out of sorts but excited. I opened my eyes in time to see him undressing and was struck at how massive his chest was as he quickly unbuttoned his shirt. He was still stacked like a body builder, but more tastefully done.

Stripping down to his Calvin's, he said, "Come here baby."

I took one step toward him, but he deftly picked me up and laid me down in the pillows. I turned onto my stomach waiting to feel his hands, but instead I felt Robert's presence leave the bed and heard him rummaging through his briefcase – then suddenly – he was back, his hands warm and firm on my calves and the back of my thighs making me moan loudly. The honey scented oil he rubbed on my body was akin to my Hanae Moré perfume; smelling almost edible. As he worked his way to my booty cheeks, he bit one, massaged the other, and then carefully removed my panties. His hands on my bum and lower back were mesmerizing; the wine, his hands, and the lowlights combined made it possible for the day to disappear and I began to drift off.

"Janie...don't fall asleep on me."

"I'm not baby," I mumbled softly.

Robert chuckled, "Damn, I know my hands work wonders, but come on baby... Wake up," he said as he spread my legs like a cop frisking a drug-dealer, sliding his hand in-between my legs all the way up to my kitty, which made me moan.

"Uhhh... I'm up now..."

"I see you're ready for me too baby. Are you? Tell me what you want me to do to you Janie."

"Kiss me Robert. Everywhere. Pull my hair. Make me moan. Make me feel you and remember you when I leave," I said urgently.

"Yes, Ma'am. You know I aim to please."

"I know." He removed my bra gently, and then put a pillow under my hips, spreading my legs a little further. I felt the heat of his breath before the wetness of his tongue made me moan, "Ahmmm."

He placed his hands under my thighs to lift me so he could assault my kitten from behind with abandon. Involuntarily, I squirmed out of reach; it was just too intense - felt like I was dissolving into a puddle of hot caramel that he was licking from the jar. He wrapped one arm around my waist to stop my escape, then he slipped his index and then his middle fingers inside me; my kitten contracted, grabbing at them greedily. Robert put his hand under my mound right on the outside of my G-Spot, then slowly screwed his fingers in and out, matching the rhythm of my hip's rotation. I couldn't help moaning with each stroke but then, he abruptly withdrew his fingers, ran his tongue from my clit to my booty and bit my cheek!

"Robert, why are you playing with me? Stop playing! You know what I want." I said, my eyes slits as I peered at him hovering above me.

"Tell me what you want Ma'am." As he said this, Robert leaned his golden brown taut muscular upper body onto mine, his weight slightly crushing my breasts against the bed. I felt his head slide from my opening, to my clit and back again and again and again…

"Hmmm…" I moaned. "I want that, baby please."

"How do you want it baby? Tell daddy how you want it – hard and fast, slow and deep? Tell me. I want to make you wet the bed baby. Make the people in the room next door wish they had peepholes." He slipped the head in slow then pulled it out quickly.

"Ah! Robert!! Please don't tease me!" I giggled breathless and tried to scoot back to make him re-enter me.

He just grabbed my hips and said, "Tell me," his voice tense with anticipation as he slid just the head in again and let it sit at my dripping opening, full penetration just out the reach of my hip's swiveling action.

"I want you!" I said loudly. "I want you every way! Make me scream and moan! Robert, please…" I said, whispering that last plea. I felt my energy dip as my longing grew in intensity.

Robert pushed past the entryway to my center, excruciatingly slow, when he reached the hilt he ground his hips pushing the head against my spot, where the pillow pushed it back towards him and said, "Hmm. I've decided to screw you first, then fuck you senseless." Robert grabbed a handful of my hair, twisted me around to face him forcing my back to arch and him deeper inside me and kissed me, wet and deep. I ground my hips against him, loving the feeling, forgetting we were not being safe; I exploded into a million bits and pieces of confetti, wetting the bed. We were just getting started.

I lay underneath his snoring weight, prone, wondering how I got to this place. How did I wind up here, in this space and this frame of mind? Torn between two men for almost two decades, knowing that my husband didn't father my son but my lover, both then and now, did. The Gomer sermon rang in my mind and through my heart as I lay there and I shifted. All of me shifted. His weight rolled off of me in the physical and I felt his place in my heart shift as well. I knew then that I was better than this. That I could be a good woman and wife, that I had to be in order to uphold the values that I held dearly but were falling so short of, especially over the past five years.

I watched him sleep, as we lay there still entangled, deeply breathing with his arm wrapped around me. I woke him, gently rubbing and shaking him, "Bobbie... Robert... We have to talk..."

"What's up?"

"I can't do this anymore."

"Do what? I know I didn't put on the condom. My bad, it was just..."

"No. This. Sleeping with you. Jon has someone following me and I can't jeopardize losing my kids. Not even for you." I said hastily climbing out of bed and reaching for my discarded panties and thigh highs. I needed to break the physical contact; the intimacy it implied was too much to bear at the moment. "Where is my garter belt?" I said absently on all fours, groping under the bed.

He threw his legs over the side of the bed abruptly without noticing me under the bed, almost kicking me senseless. "What the hell do you mean?"

I fell back on my behind and looked up at him, "I can't risk him leaving me and taking the kids Robert. He has evidence and grounds for divorce with JD's blood work not matching. I can't. I just can't live without my babies Bobbie." I stood up and pulled on my garter and underwear.

Robert pulled on his underwear and as I went to pull on my skirt, he grabbed my upper arms, pulling me to him. "You don't have to Janine. We can make it happen. Together. Don't you have faith in me? I thought you loved me…" he let me go, brusquely putting his hands over his face, then running them through his hair.

I stopped getting dressed and looked at him, but he avoided my gaze. "I do. But I've built a life with Jon. Our children know him as their dad. That's all they know. I can't take that away from them; a divorce would ruin their lives much less mine, and my reputation. Did you forget that I work in my church community? This would be unforgiveable. I would lose my position and the non-profit I created!"

"All of that is more important to you than me?" He asked as he turned his back on me and swiftly buttoned up his trousers then pulled on his shirt.

"It's not like that Robert. I just… I just can't anymore. I just can't. Don't you understand?"

"No, Janine. I don't."

I didn't know what else to say. There were so many questions buzzing around in my head, '*Did he know he was JD's dad? Was he going to try to stop us from staying together if he did know? Why did he come to the hospital that day after just sleeping with me only two hours before?*' All I could think was that I needed out. Now. There was too much at stake. Even after he showed me the pictures with Leslie, I still couldn't leave Jon. I felt like I deserved it. I was cheating with him after all. Right?

We left the hotel room in strained silence. Robert refused to touch or speak to me on the elevator down, but I could feel the heat coming off of him in waves. He was beyond pissed. He was hurt and there was really nothing I could do to stop the pain this time. I had to save my family; no matter what, this had to stop.

I had a lot on my mind and had no plans on going back to work after I left that sordid scene. I usually would stop by the Prime Town Center Gym where this guy who looked exactly like Robert worked, and take a shower – I have a membership there even though I don't go like I should. But Jon was picking up Amber, which meant I was free until evening, so I went to do some retail therapy instead.

I was trying on some shoes in Nordstrom's, when I got a call from some detective agency. The receptionist stated that there were some new developments in my case and that I needed to come to their offices immediately, so that I could speak to the lead agent on it. I knew Jon had me under surveillance, but wasn't sure why I was being made privy to any of the goings on, as I was the subject of the investigation. In any case, my uneasiness gave way to my curiosity and I asked the lady when I should come in and was surprised by her response.

"We need to have you come in this evening."

"But it's already 4 PM Ms. …" I said wondering how late is too late to see an investigator.

"Agatha, Ms. Agatha."

"Okay, so what time would I be coming in to see your lead agent, Ms. Agatha?"

"6 PM is his next available opening for today. I won't be in the office, but you will be buzzed in directly. Push code #1112 so that the phone will ring into his office and not to my desk and he will let you in himself."

"Who am I going to be meeting with Ms. Agatha?"

"Oh! I never did say, did I?" She chuckled. You will be meeting with the owner of Douglass Detective

Agency, Robert Matthews. Please be on time dearheart. Goodbye," she said and promptly hung up in my ear.

I sat there dumbfounded. My lover, whose bed I just left, is requesting a meeting with me and come to find out, he's the one investigating me for my husband.

CHAPTER 9

Jon: Take That, Take That

I got back home from seeing JD at the rehab, grabbed a beer out of the fridge and turned on the game. I have to admit that I was glad that I had dropped my babygirl at her Godmother's house because I felt like drinking and thinking. Even though Mishie was sick, she really wanted to see Amber a lot lately. I guess she wanted to get her time in and plant some lasting memories.

I realized as I sat there in front of the big screen, sipping and barely watching the Celtics kill the Knicks in a classic game, that what Neene's done doesn't change how I feel when I see her. I want to hate her ass so bad, want to hurt her, make her feel like I do when I look at her... The war going on in my heart and mind is driving me crazy. How could she do this to me? To us? I can't wait for Robert to give me all the intel he has on her, I mean come on man... What would make her do that? I have given her all that I have... All that I am. I trusted Neene, wanted her to be my wife from the moment I laid eyes on her and that hasn't changed even with my knowing that my son, isn't mine. Disgusted with my life, I got up and made myself a sandwich. I couldn't keep drinking on an empty stomach.

When I went to see JD today, it was heartbreaking; he wouldn't even speak to me. I came into the room and he turned his back on me. It made me wonder if he knew he wasn't mine too. The doctor said it may be like that, where he would ignore us when we came to visit, but I know that he's talked to Neene, because she said he told her he didn't want his friends to see him like that, to tell them to just call him instead.

When she came in tonight, I was waiting for her in the living room. I had to do something to break this pain I was feeling. It felt like my prayers were going unanswered and instead my worst nightmares were coming true. I was sitting in my favorite leather armchair facing the doorway with a half empty bottle of Patron in my hand, so drunk, my coherency surprised even me.

"Where are you coming from Neene? Come here, let me smell you - Just stop right there and take those panties off," I sneered, startling her as she walked into the door.

"What?" she replied, eyes all big. "Come on Jon. I just walked in the door. I am too tired for this!"

"I don't give a flying fuck Neene. Take them panties off and toss them here so I can smell them."

"Jon...," Neene sucked her teeth, "Why you tripping?" she whined, as she lifted her tailored skirt above her black lace garter, stuck her finger in the waistband of her thong and threw it in my face. "There! You happy drunky?" she said sarcastically, standing there with a smirk on her face.

I inhaled her scent and was instantly rock-hard. "Humph. You think you slick huh?" I chuckled and put her underwear in my pocket. "Now shut up, keep them heels on and bring that ass over here right the hell now," I said slowly, words sliding together slightly.

"What d'ya want Jon? Come on man. I am not up for all this bullcrap tonight," she said trying to walk past me to go upstairs. "All I want to do is go to bed Jon. Stop playing all the damn time," she said exasperated.

I grabbed her arm and pulled her into my lap.

"Get off of me Jon!"

"Shut up before you wake the baby," I was so gone, I'd forgotten Amber wasn't even home. "You gonna give me mine tonight," I said through clenched teeth, then licked her neck.

"Yours? Yours! Really Jon? If that's the case, why are we going through all of this therapy crap then?" she asked.

Grabbing a handful of her hair, I shoved my tongue in her mouth in response. I started to knead her breast roughly, kissing her 'til she moaned, then I shoved my hand up her skirt and rubbed her clit until I felt her wet my hand. I stopped myself from going any further, I couldn't take it from her; I wanted her to give it to me. But then Neene said my name in that quiet breathless way she does when she's about to start beggin' for me and I lost it. By the time I realized what was happening, her pearl buttons were scattered all over the living room floor, her right bra strap was popped and her skirt was ripped up the back split. I was knee deep into my wife in the middle of the living room floor.

Neene was so wet and ready for me; I prayed it was love and not familiarity. She dug her nails in my back and began to grind her hips into each thrust I made, but she was also crying softly as she came. I could feel her kitten spazzing on my stiffness while simultaneously hearing her sob, "I'm sorry Jon, forgive me. I'm so sorry. I love you, Jon, I love you so much," in my ear. I wanted to stop, her crying was killing me… but couldn't until I let it go. Yeah… Tonight was crazy. I kinda feel like I went too far, but how can I? She's still my wife.

I woke up in my chair with my boxer's on and a mean headache. I didn't believe what I did, I mean, the

85

sex good as all get out, but I didn't want it to go down like that. I will say this – It showed me one thing I really needed to know; my wife loves me.

I got up and went into the kitchen to get something to drink. My throat felt like I had been gargling sand. My head was so heavy and dull, I didn't even realize that I had been dragging my jeans with me to the kitchen by one leg until I opened the fridge door and happened to look down. Damn, talk about a hot mess. I checked the time – 2 AM. I wonder if Marcus is up…

"Hey man… What's up? You alright? Where you at?" Marcus answered, sounding like he was wide-awake, thank God.

"I'm home…," I replied slowly.

"What's going on? Uh… You and Neene alright?" he asked hesitantly.

"Nah man. I think I just effed up real bad," I said sitting at the kitchen island with my head on my forearm, the cool marble a comfortable distraction from the turmoil bubbling in my gut.

"What did you do?"

"I took it from her Marc…"

"Took it!" he asked surprised. "What do you mean took it? You didn't force her to have sex did you?"

"Man, I don't even know if I really took it or not, but her clothes are all over the living room floor ripped and I remember being mad as hell before she came in…"

"Jon, this is going too damn far now. First JD, then the therapist, now this… Wait. Did she call the police?" Marcus asked, fear making his baritone tremble.

"No."

"Whew..." he exhaled, slowly. "Okay… So, maybe you didn't do as much as you think. Were you drunk?" he asked relieved.

"Yeah. I was done. I'd been drinking beer all day and had a fifth of Patron sitting in the easy chair thinking about everything that was going on and when I saw her walk in the door, I just lost it."

"That's crazy man."

"All I remember is how good it was to be with her again and her crying while she said she loved me."

"Umm… Maybe it's not so bad then. Have you gone upstairs yet?"

"Nah."

"What you gonna do?"

"I don't know yet. That's why I called you."

"Jon. Go talk to your wife. That's the one thing you haven't done yet."

"I don't know what to say Marcus. I really don't. I feel like she should be crawling on her hands and knees begging me to take her back, but she's not and its making me crazy."

"Dude. You think she doesn't know about your dirt?" he asked cynically.

"Whatchu mean?" I was shocked! "I mean, what does Neene know? How?" I got up and started pacing the kitchen floor, trailing that same one pants leg. Damn.

"Mishie makes it seems like Janine knows more about what you have been doing than you think. She ain't tell me everything they talked about, but you better be ready to face the music if you want your marriage."

"You know damn well I didn't cheat on her! I wanted to cheat on her ass so bad, but I couldn't do it."

"What about Leslie, Jon? Come on man," he said, his tone mocking me slightly. "What about your other son. I haven't breathed a word of it to Mishie, but come on man who are you fooling?"

"Marc, man, when I told Leslie what was going on with Neene and me, she practically put her kitten on a silver platter for me, but I couldn't see myself starting something up with her. All I could do was laugh and shake my head; I mean I was helping her out because she had my son, but there was nothing between us; not really then and hasn't really been anything going on with us since I married Neene."

"Why should Janine believe you? To be honest, it's crazy hard for me to even believe that all those years of you going down there you haven't broken her off. I mean – did Leslie ever get married?"

"No… but what's even crazier is my sons' are almost identical and I was downtown that day with Jacob when Jon Jr. had his car accident."

"What!" he practically screamed into my ear, and then I heard Michelle's voice in the background calling Marcus. She sounded so weak that it finally hit me, he was nursing his sick wife and all of my drama was just adding to his burden.

"Look Marcus, my bad calling so late. I appreciate you my dude. I'll work it all out; take care of your wife man. Kiss the kids man, we'll talk," then I just hung up.

It was about 3 AM when I ventured toward the bedroom. I'd been sleeping in the guest room and realized that it was time I went back where I belonged, in bed with my wife.

CHAPTER 10
Robert: Busted and Disgusted

I sat at my desk with my head pounding and my thoughts racing. I thought I was slick. I had the girl and mostly the life I wanted, but that niggah Jon seemed to still have the upper hand after all these years. First Leslie, then Janine and then just when I thought I would be able to get Janine back, it all falls to pieces. I investigated him and showed Neene what he was doing with that chick Leslie and she still wouldn't leave his ass. All she had to say was, "It serves me right. All these years of loving you the way I do, and being his wife… We should have never gotten married… But we used to be happy, until you came home anyway."

I couldn't believe where she was going with this. I said, "Come on Neene. Are you fo'sho gonna let this niggah play you like this? I can take care of you and the kids wit' outta problem."

She had the nerve to say, "No, you can't. He's the only father they know… I know I need to go back to Jon to stay – Bobby, I feel like I am living a lie just waiting to be exposed. I don't know how much longer I can live like this."

"Live like what?" Is what the hell I really wanted to know – 'Having a real man that loves you, wants you and understands you? Doesn't take you for granted or abuse your affection and time? I didn't understand it. Why does she feel like she owes him when he has another woman in North Carolina that he takes care of and splits his time with?' I just looked at her and shook my head. I wondered if she knew her own worth. I wish I could have shown her pics of him in a compromising position with Leslie, but he was either real careful or he wasn't really hittin' that, but I doubt that seriously. I kept the pictures of the kid he had with Leslie out of it, I didn't want to break Neene's heart, but now I'm thinking I should just blow the whistle on his ass.

I pulled out a picture of her I kept in my desk drawer. She was so happy – she was beaming at me holding the camera and I could see the love in her eyes. Her hair was all long and pretty, almost to her waist and she was so small and fragile. I had another one by my bed at home of us when we were youngins – I missed those times together. It seemed like it was so long ago and such a short time together now.

She used to write me in prison and I could tell she was lonely from the things she didn't say. I mean, before all this, Neene knew better than to rub her relationship with Jon in my face, but when she talked about how she was home with JD by herself all the time while he was out making his fortune, I knew she wanted someone there at night. She told me about her and Mishie hangin' out all the time while JD was at school and then her building a shelter with her church so that she could contribute to the house and not be so bored while he was away for three-four days a week. I remember thinking that I will be there to fill those days soon enough. When she came to see me on trial, I felt this love that I haven't been able to let go of since. She only came a few times and the last time she came, she brought JD with her. I guess she didn't have a sitter for him. Even then he reminded me of myself when I was a youngin'. Now with my blood being a match, I know he's mine for real, which means I am fighting for the family I should have had.

As soon as I got out, I checked my real estate investments and made sure that the complex I built my PI business in was owned by me through some dummy corporations that did not accept bids on the development project so I could handpick my contractors; excluding Jon and Marcus' business and shareholders altogether. I felt bad doing that to Marcus… He actually came to see me in prison a few times just to check up on me and make sure I was good and didn't need anything. He didn't have to though because my aunt Aggie had my back the whole time I was down. She sent me packages from her own money and managed my affairs for me while I was in the pen. Aunt Aggie even came up on the bus to see me! I told her I didn't want her to see me like that, but she came once a month like clockwork anyway. She told me, "Bobby baby, we is all we got and we got 'ta take good care a one 'nother 'cause no one else's gointa to do it."

That Auntie Aggie ain't never let me down.

CHAPTER 11
Jon: The (Half) Confession

I went upstairs and stood outside our bedroom door listening to Janine crying, not sure of what I could do to bring the situation around. I knew I was wrong and I knew she was wrong, but I wasn't sure about how to make things right again. I just wanted things to be the way they were when we were happy. I just wasn't sure if it was all a lie, then I remembered something that Bishop had given us when we did our pre-marital counseling. He had given me: Proverbs 2:16-19, "Wisdom will save you also from the adulterous woman, from the wayward woman with her seductive words, who has left the partner of her youth and ignored the covenant she made before God. Surely her house leads down to death and her paths to the spirits of the dead. None who go to her return or attain the paths of life…" and given Janine: Proverbs 31:10-12, "A wife of noble character who can find? She is worth far more than rubies. Her husband has full confidence in her and lacks nothing of value. She brings him good, not harm, all the days of her life." In essence, he'd given me the verses about the Wayward Woman and Janine about the perfect wife. It was one of our homework assignments; we had to study them and e-mail the Bishop what qualities we thought a wife would have.

I remembered that they were in my bedside bible and I thought that I could maybe show them to her to make her remember the good times. So, I went in, turned on my side of the bed's lamp, and pulled them out of my bible.

"Hey babe… Janine," I whispered.

"Yes Jon," she replied quietly.

"Look at this," I said as I handed her the two assignment sheets.

"You've kept them all these years?" she replied.

"Yup. Remember how we switched the papers and laughed at the Wayward Woman verses. We just knew that wasn't who you were, but you were…" I said quietly then added quickly, "I mean you used to be… but I still know that you are a Proverbs 31 woman too."

"I can't be both Jon," she replied rolling her eyes, grabbing some tissue off her side's nightstand and wiping them.

"Yes, you can Neene. We are not all dark or light, all good or bad, but we are all human though and prone to make mistakes. I'm human too babe. I know I'm 'Deacon Dupont' and all that, but I'm also just Jon from BK too; I walk that line and fight that fight between my old and new man all the time. I just fight to be strong in the face of doing what's easy or what feels good at the moment."

"So do I Jon. That's why I apologized in our first discussion about this whole thing."

"I know, but I have faith that you can choose to fully be that Proverbs 31 wife, not just on the surface of things – what I need to know is whether *you want* to be that for real or not, because if not, I can't stay in this marriage. I'm going crazy."

"I get that. I just have one question for you that I need addressed before I can even begin to decide what I want to do about us."

"What's that?"

"What about Leslie?"

"Who?" I asked. I was tripping, but playing it off cool. What exactly did she know about Leslie?

"You know exactly who I'm talking about Jon, don't play dumb."

"You mean Les from school?" I said coolly. "What about her?"

"Jon," Janine said looking at me sideways.

"What Janine?" I asked trying to sound innocent staring at the wall behind her head. I didn't know what she knew and I didn't expect for this to come out now. Marcus was right. What am I going to say? In my mind, I was scrambling for an excuse or a witty comeback that would steer us away from a conversation about Leslie and what had been happening for the past almost 19 years behind my wife's back.

"Jon. Look. At. Me.," she sat up clutching the pillow she was just lying on and stared at me intently.

I didn't respond. I didn't even look in her face.

"So! *You* make me go to therapy to save *our* marriage, make *me* out to be this brazen harlot of a wife, but *you*, you don't even want to talk about *Leslie*!" she hissed, clenching the poor pillow in a vice grip, pointed nails digging into it mercilessly, her eyes rimmed red and black from the tears with mascara sliding onto her cheeks.

I was scared, I wanted to say something, but what was there to say? It was obvious she knew something, but I wasn't sure what and I wasn't ready to admit that I had been unfaithful. I mean, not in the same way she had been, but I *was* going between two homes.

"What do you want me to say Janine? I found out that my son wasn't mine when I needed to help him the most and I still haven't figured out why the hell Robert

95

was in the hospital with him when I wasn't! What the hell do you want from me?" I shouted, skirting the issue.

"You know what Jon? You just said a mouthful, but you didn't answer my question. I already know about Leslie, so you can act crazy if you want to, but we will be splitting everything 50-50," she said calmly rolling her eyes, then gave me her back to stare at in disbelief, as she got herself comfortable again in bed.

I sat there for a minute contemplating where we were and my part in how we got here. Made me wonder if I was the reason Janine stepped out to begin with, if she knew about Leslie and my son before she started cheating, or if she was cheating from the beginning. But on the real, the one thing that kept bugging me was that I wanted to know who fathered my son. But how could I force her to tell me that, when I have a son with Leslie? We were at an impasse.

"Janine," I whispered rubbing her shoulder.

"What Jon?" She replied, snatching away from me.

"You said you loved me and that you were sorry..."

"So, what Jon. That has nothing to do with what we're talking about now."

I took a deep breath and tried to calm myself and said what I knew would at least diffuse the situation for now, "I just wanted to say that I'm sorry too and I love you," I said, my voice choked with real emotion. I didn't want to lose my wife and children or face my own betrayal publically, I couldn't.

Janine hesitated and her shoulders rose and fell as she cried; after a few agonizing minutes she slowly turned to face me with tears still rolling from the corners of her eyes, "I know Jon. That's why I'm still here lying next to you."

I didn't reply, I just took my wife into my arms and made love to her slowly, kissing every inch of her body until she begged for me to be inside of her.

When I awoke that morning and got ready to go see Robert, I checked my messages and found that Dr. Williams called me and left one saying that it was time I joined the sessions, but I didn't want to. It seemed like something may come out that I'm not ready to discuss with Neene. Matter of fact, I know it will. They have met 3 times and I am supposed to join in for the next 3 sessions as the husband or partner, whatever she said, but I wonder what would happen if I just called her and said I didn't want to come.

"Good afternoon, Dr. Williams' office," the receptionist's clipped tone was brisk and all business.

"Hello, this is Mr. Dupont. Is it possible for me to speak with Dr. Williams in reference to my office visit later this week?"

"She is unable to come to phone at this time. Would you like to leave a message?"

"Um…," I hesitated unsure of what to say, after all I was the one who set this up. "Well… Can you please tell her that I will not be able to attend the sessions with my wife? Janine Dupont."

"I will let her know as soon as she's available. She will still want to speak with you. What is a number where you can be reached?"

"404-352-1276," I said thinking about what the hell she would want to *speak to me* about. I'm the one who pays for her services and if I don't want to partake in the sessions, I don't have to and neither she nor Janine can make me.

CHAPTER 12
Janine: Transgressions

I arrived at Dr. Williams' office this week thinking that it was going to be ugly when I told her what I did. Sleeping with my husband and then Robert twice, even if it was one of those times was against my will, all in one day even sounds bad to my own jaded ears, especially in light of the change I am supposed to be focused on. I walked in that office feeling like she could smell the other man's sweat coming from my pores.

"It's nice to see you today Janine"

"You too, Dr. Williams"

"How are you doing with staying focused on your goal to put your marriage and husband before yourself?"

"I don't know Dr. Williams. It turns out that it is much more difficult than I thought it would be. I've already slept with my other man twice since we last met," I stated this matter-of-factly with the expectation that she would explode or be angry, some kind of reaction but, nothing.

Just her cool, calm and collected, looking at me steadily, then softly saying, "Ok. How do you feel about that?"

"I don't know how to feel. I feel somewhat ashamed, but not so much, more like disappointed that I can't keep a promise to myself." I will admit that I was disappointed in her lack of response to my transgressions, but I guess being a professional, if she were to react like that, it would be judgmental, which she cannot be. Good.

"So, the promise you are trying to keep is to yourself?"

"Yes and no… I guess… I to be honest I really don't know Doctor. I feel like I should be able to say I am going to stop sleeping with other men and that be what I do, but it's so much more complicated than that. I can't risk there being problems for my family so, I have to do things slowly."

"So, I am hearing you say that you feel your family is a part of that promise? I ask because you said yes and no."

"Yes, they are part of the promise, my husband in particular, but my children as well. I don't want Amber and Jon Jr. to view their mother as a whore who slept around on their father!"

"Would they think that? Do you feel like that about yourself?"

I was silenced by her question. It stopped me in my tracks. I didn't see myself as a whore, but if someone outside myself looked at what I was doing, I couldn't say they wouldn't. Maybe I was. "No Dr. Williams, I don't feel like I am a whore. Maybe I should, but I don't. I just feel caught up."

"Don't should on yourself, Janine. It's a values call. If what you value is sexual pleasure and the values of society-at-large are different, it's the judgment that's unhealthy. What you need to be sure of is that your values match your partner's values, so that no one is hurt. You

100

said another sexual partner, the one other than your husband… Tell me more about that."

I wasn't sure I wanted to… I did bring it up so perhaps I do, but… Who am I kidding?! I need to get this off my chest. "As soon as I left here, I had to meet with Robert, my now ex-lover."

"Had to?"

"Well, I guess I didn't have to, but I didn't want to leave him cold and have some repercussions or stalker backlash, plus I was hungry and was headed to where we would have met anyway."

"Oh… Okay."

"So, I got there and we met, ate some, talked and went upstairs to our regular room. He told me he loved me and wanted to help me raise my children…"

"Did he say that before, during or after you went upstairs to the room?" she interrupted abruptly.

"Way before we even discussed going upstairs and after we made love actually. Why?"

"The throes of passion can lead people to say disingenuous things. The fact that he said it when you were eating, and before he knew you would be having sex, may mean that he actually believes he does. How does that make you feel? Him loving you?"

"I don't know. I love Robert and I love what he does to my body – he is an excellent lover, and knows me well, but he is not who I want to spend my life with. We have absolutely nothing in common except time invested and memories shared…"

"Is Jon who you want to spend your life with? Does Jon appreciate all of you?" She asked quietly.

I took a moment to ponder that, I mean Jon knows about my adulterous ways and is still willing to work things out. "Jon knows me, but not as well as Robert to be honest. He never really took the time to really know me well even though we have been married for almost 20 years."

"How do you feel about that?" she asked softly.

"I don't know. Who knows what he does when he is away on business, but he's always made me feel like he still loves me, cares for me and wants me… Always, even if he doesn't know me as well."

"Tell me more about that, how does he make you feel that," the doctor asked quietly.

"Well, because while he is away on business during the week, Jon always manages to call at least twice a day to speak to only me; we have our morning and late night talk. He also talks to the kids when they get home from school during his 6 pm call. I used to make our moments alone sexy and talk a little dirty to him on our early morning talk, because I know how much he loves to roll over onto me in the morning, but I began thinking that I may be getting him too hot and bothered while he was so far away, I had to stop," I said shaking my head.

"Tell me more about thinking you had to stop," she probed gently.

"I just thought that I would be getting him hot for the next woman. I just started to get kind of suspicious of him and thought there may be someone else in North Carolina. He changed his routine slightly and I was hypersensitive to changes like that after Robert and Jesus; the only men I ever loved, betrayed me with another woman."

"Really?… You just said 'the only men I ever loved' when referring to Robert and Jesus. Did you realize you said that?" she asked pointedly.

"What? I said that?" I was shocked. "I meant to say the only other men I ever loved doc! I love my husband, but it was never the way I feel about Robert."

"Feel about Robert… Or felt about Robert," she said looking into my eyes expectantly. She paused for about two whole minutes waiting for me to elaborate but… There was nothing to say. I still loved Robert even after he betrayed me and took from me what was no longer his.

"I want you to think about what I am about to say to you and give me an answer in our next session – Do you think that you are capable of being monogamous? I know this is one of our shorter sessions because you have a pressing engagement, but I have an assignment for you. I want you to think of everyone else involved in *every* decision you make, *before* you think about yourself; be it what to watch on TV, to what you cook for dinner, then journal at night how those decisions felt and bring the journal with you for our next session." She went to her desk and handed me a paisley fabric bound journal. "Okay?"

"Sure Doc. Thanks again and see you later," I said quickly as I gathered my oversized pale gold leather Gucci bag, placed the journal inside of it and shaded my eyes and thoughts; I don't know how much I can tell her about what is going on with Robert and I.

I adjusted my orange, green and multi shaded gold Gucci scarf in the mirrored reflection of the door and rushed out. I had to meet with Michelle for lunch. I made this our day, instead of Friday to fill the void of seeing Kirk. Michelle missed lunch last Friday because of chemo and I was wondering how she was fairing through all of this. She told me she did not want me to come with her and even though I insisted and even had Marcus get it on my plea she wanted to do this all by herself. Talk about brave and strong. My best friend was the strongest woman I knew.

I walked into the Cornbread Cafe looking for her to be where we usually sat, by the window so we could people watch and chat while we ate, but I didn't see her. She is never late so I assumed that she was seated elsewhere due to the business of the cafe, but when I looked closer, I noticed a well-dressed woman, in a booth near our regular seat, in oversized Chanel shades and a black and white Chanel logo scarf tightly tied onto her head; it was Michelle. I hadn't seen her except in passing over the past three weeks because of being at the hospital with JD, but that short time hollowed her cheeks tremendously. I mean, damn! I picked up Amber from her house so many times over this whole ordeal, but looking at her out where we hang out she looked so other than the Mishie I remember from just last month. I felt so guilty for neglecting her with all that was going on in my life, hers was slipping away almost unnoticed and it was heartbreaking. To have her judge me and look at me in shock and disgust would kill me; I already felt dead inside. I swallowed my self-pity and resolved to focus only on Michelle today.

"Hey girl!" I said trying to sound cheerful, failing wretchedly.

"What's up Neene?" Michelle stated coolly as she took off her shades and looked into my eyes.

"N-n-n-nothing," I stammered feeling my face flush.

"Really? I would have thought a whole fucking lot was up with my godson in the hospital and your ass going to therapy, Chica. So are you gonna come clean or am I gonna have to tell *you* what's up?" She replied matter of fact, staring me straight in the face.

"Come on Michelle – damn... You obviously know my mess is unraveling, but I am not here to talk about me. What is going on with you babygirl?" Are you okay? What's up with the chemo? What are the doctors saying about recovery?" I hit her with rapid-fire questions hoping it would take her off my jacked up set of circumstances. It didn't.

"You already know what is happening to me Neene, I am coming apart slow. The scarf is hiding my patches of hair and the glasses – the hollows in my face. Neither is doing a great job, but shit, I am trying to be that diva I am inside and will be, to the bitter end." She chuckled heartily, then sobered up – "Chick, you better spill it cause I ain't got much time left to dawdle over things we have no control. You on the other hand, have to fix this mess you got yourself in, and quick."

I didn't know what to say. I sat there and looked at this woman I have known since girlhood – shoot she was my first kiss! To see her emaciated, but still strong, while I had the gift of health, but was weak-willed, gave me courage to tell her. Plus, she probably knew most of the story anyway.

"How much do you know anyway?" I asked as I took off my shades and put them in the case, avoiding her glare. I already knew my husband confided in Marcus about everything but I didn't know how much he would tell, the male ego is a fragile, temperamental entity and I doubt he wanted to let Marcus know the extent of my betrayal.

"Chica you know, I knew that hospital scene was bound to happen. I – ," she stopped short of what we both knew.

"Whatever Mishie, you and that Karma crap need to stop. I almost lost everything in that hospital room," I added quietly. Michelle bought the pregnancy test 18 years ago and waited patiently for me to come out of the bathroom after bawling for what seemed a lifetime. She tried to get me to tell Jon and Robert or at least one of them the truth, but I passed on all that. I was going to have the life I always wanted. Period.

"No, for real Neene! JD has been so healthy – no broken bones or anything, come to think about it this is the first time he has had more than a slight cold since he's been born! Must be Robert's genes' cause that damn Jon stays sick," she laughed lightly and added, "Everything has to come out one way or another babe."

"Don't make fun Mishie. It's messed up enough without you cracking slick! Damn!" I said hotly, and then added, "Did you order already? I am hungry as a hostage!"

"Nope. Not hungry; just came to talk to you love."

Just then, our waitress Marie, comes up and says, "Are you lovely ladies ready to order? Should I bring your regulars?"

"Yes." I said quickly, and then turned back to Mishie.

"Remember when we were 12, up on our roof – how I said that I wanted a man that would never leave?"

"Yes." Mishie said quietly.

"Well, that is what Jon represented to me even with his holier-than-thou ways. You know he has a woman in North Carolina right? He is Deacon Dupont, but at the same time he's been cheating on me religiously."

"Yes, I know," she replied gently, "but does two wrongs make a right? You married Jon out of hurt and revenge, not out of love. You wanted Robert and obviously you have never stopped wanting him."

"I broke it off with Robert, Mish, I still love him, but I love my husband too; and it's just not in my heart anymore to be with anyone but my husband. I realized it when I felt dirty the other night; Robert forced himself on me after I pleaded with him not to. I said no...."

"Wait! *He forced himself on you!* Come on Neene. Why didn't you call the police?" She asked shaking her head with her eyes wide.

"I feel like I asked for it Mishie; I led him on all these years, but when it comes down to it – I love Jon, we have history and built a life together that I just can't throw away so easily. Plus, he's the only father my children know and love. Robert and I picked back up when he came home from jail about five years ago, I don't know how he did it, but he just showed up at my job and took me to lunch," I said, sounding as if I were still confused about how it happened.

"How did he know where you worked?" she asked surprised.

"I was writing him in jail, but it wasn't really much of anything to the letters. I did tell him I was building a shelter to work in part-time through my church, but not which one."

"*Girl*! Writing him in jail! You know that man is a detective! Wait... Was he back then? That was like 5 years ago. Have you been sleeping with him all this time?"

"Not exactly," I stated quietly. "It was platonic at first, just filling the time while Jon was away."

"Oh. My. Lord. Neene," she said sadly shaking her head. "You never even said anything to me. Is Amber his too?"

"I don't know, to be honest. At first we were safe, but then things got real relaxed Mishie. I just don't know what to do anymore."

"Me either," she replied, shaking her scarf clad head.

"Come on Mishie. I broke up with Robert, but honestly, he was my best friend. You know I went to all of his early court dates and everything."

"I went with you to one, I didn't know you went back though."

"Yeah. I did because I felt bad; I watched his career tank with all the rumors, drug use and trades. I saw all of those supermodels he dated after we broke up and wondered why not one of them or his family was at his court dates. His aunt was there at one point, so I stopped going because I saw he had some support... I loved him, but I had to focus on my husband."

"When and why did you pick back up with him then?"

"I was lonely, Jon is gone so much and sometimes he doesn't come home for weeks. I began to really want Robert, he was the only man I thought really loved me. He was so hurt when I told him I was going back to Jon."

"Humph," she snorted, "He sure has a funny way of showing it. Marcus told me your husband hired Robert to investigate you. Now that I know all of this – I don't know what to think... Why would he take the job?"

"He's blackmailing me to sleep with him again, that's why! Robert said he would tell Jon about us, said he'd make it seem like I have been sleeping with him for our entire marriage. Why won't he just let me go," I said covering my face with my hands trying to cover the tears that were streaming down my face.

Marie returned silently with our food and the aroma of my BBQ Shrimp and Grits made me momentarily forget all about my drama. I was starving, so I wiped my eyes and dove into my plate without giving my situation another thought.

I watched Mishie take one look at her French Toast, and a look of absolute revulsion passed over her face; she promptly excused herself.

"What in the world?" I thought to myself and then I remembered somberly, *'Chemo.'*

She returned about 15 minutes later, paler than when she left and sat down heavily. *Well, as heavily as she could at 110 pounds.'* I thought to myself inwardly cringing at the sight of her gaunt frame.

I wanted to ask her what happened, but instead tried to crack a joke, "I was about to come in there and get you thought maybe you flushed yourself down the toilet."

She said, "Well. I will say that I almost did and it wasn't pretty to say the least." She cracked a smile, then turned serious quickly saying, "This chemo, coupled with the losing my appetite and hair is trying my patience. I thought I might be able to at least look at the food…"

"It will pass. God knows I need you more than He does," I stated matter-of-factly, as I ate the last bite of my cheddar grits.

She smiled slightly, and then looking in my face and pointing towards the sky said, "Have you talked to Him lately about what you're going through or are you going to try to get through this without Him? I know I haven't been as present in church as I should, but God's love is ever present. Why haven't you tried praying your way through the loneliness and shame? Or at least for an answer to what troubles you most – Should you leave your husband for good and be with Robert, who we both know you love or commit to making your marriage work?"

"I can't even think about that right now Misch for real. I want to know what is up with you! You seemed like you were getting better a couple of weeks ago and now you've lost more weight and can't even stand the smell of your favorite food! What did the doctor say today?"

"Well... They told me that they wanted to stop the chemo for a few weeks last time because it had spread to my lymph nodes and they wanted to make sure it didn't metastasize into any other organs, but it back fired."

"Wait? What? What do you mean it back fired Mishie?"

"When I went today, they said that I've gone from Stage II to Stage IV and that it has spread to one of my kidneys and maybe my liver. They gave me a chemo treatment right then and there, hence my inability to even stand the smell of my food." She shook her head and looked at me soberly, "Janine, I'm really dying."

"No. You're not. We just have to find another doctor Misch. And we are going to sue their ass at this office too for stopping the treatment!"

"No, we are not going to sue. Calm down Janine, the doctor explained that sometimes stopping the treatment could also stop the spread of the cancer into other body parts. This time it didn't work. We knew the risk; Marcus and I discussed it for a couple days before we decided to go ahead and stop the chemo treatments."

"So, why did you seem better? I'm not understanding Mishie." Disgusted, I pushed my plate away and braced myself for an explanation that wouldn't change anything.

"Because at first, the symptoms caused by the chemo subsided, which allowed me to eat and feel normal for a little while, but then the pain in my back started," her voice trailed off, so I looked up to see what caught her attention. She was looking out of the window where there was a couple walking down the street holding hands; she watched them until they were out of sight. As I watched them with her, I felt like I was slowly disappearing as they faded out of our line of sight. She was my anchor. I was always the wild one; dating bad boys, bar-tending, hip-hop star tripping, and she was my voice of reason, my rock. Now, here she was drifting away and there was nothing I could do to keep her here.

CHAPTER 13
Jon: Deja Vu

I went to the rehab facility today to sit with JD while he got ran through the paces by this new therapist. It's funny because he reminds me of someone, but I just can't place it right now. In any case, he's really good. He's pushing JD to overcome his depression about playing ball by telling him about other athletes and how they have overcome similar injuries and gone on to be Olympians, like Oscar Pistonrius and Ryan McIntosh. Wait. That gives me a great idea! I'm going to get pictures of those athletes and create oversized framed portraits for his bedroom and our workout room in the basement, which is about to become JD's personal home rehab. As a matter of fact, I need to ask this dude what equipment I needed to add to our home gym to make it work.

"Hey man, thanks for doing such a great job with JD," I said walking over to where they were working on some parallel bars.

Kirk Jones walked across the small workout room to meet me half way and reached his hand out for me to shake it, "No problem. He's a good kid and from what he's told me, he's nice at basketball too."

"Yeah, just like me when I was his age," I replied shaking his hand firmly, then turned to my son and asked, "How you feelin' JD?"

"I'm aight dad, just a little sore. Where's mom? She was here with me last Thursday..."

"Well, she wanted to catch up at work and told me she wanted me to come and encourage you on Thursdays until you come home. Speaking of coming home, I know he has a few weeks, Kirk, but what do I need to add to my home gym?"

"You probably don't need to add anything actually. You have a treadmill, an elliptical and an exercise bike right?" Kirk assured.

"Yup. And I have a pull-up bar, a set of free weights and a bench too!" I replied excited to already be prepared for JD's return home.

"I was getting ready to ask you if you had a pull-up bar!" He laughed, "JD will need that to build more upper body strength, so he still can get around on his own while learning how to maneuver with his new limb."

"So, is this the one he will have permanently?" I asked concerned, watching JD slowly walk over to a treadmill and walk methodically on it while the incline changed every two minutes keeping him on point.

"Nah. He will have this one about four to six months and with his growth, he will probably need a different one before he goes to college and perhaps another one either junior or senior year," Kirk responded.

"You seem really familiar to me. I am trying to place you but I can't," I laughed.

"Dad, he looks just like uncle Rob," JD said concentrating on staying upright on the ever-changing slope of the treadmill.

I don't know why that riled me, but it gave me an uneasy feeling to have their resemblance be so strong that even JD saw it. He really was a shorter, younger version of Robert when I took a long good look at him, and it was unhinging. I tried to laugh it off, "Boy, when's the last time you saw uncle Rob? You must have been 6 years old!"

"Nah, he's been to the hospital to see me on days you and mom couldn't come. He just came and sat on the side though, didn't really talk to me too much, but I didn't want to talk anyway so it was cool."

"Word?" I asked.

"Yup, he said he'd donated some blood and wanted to make sure it didn't kill me," JD laughed, then added, "It was funny for some reason when he said that." Then he moved into a new exercise Kirk had him doing.

I didn't know how to take this new information. Robert and I hadn't been close for a really long time and even though he was with me when I found out, he didn't ask me if he could come and see JD. Maybe he talked to Neene? Or maybe it was part of his investigation? I doubt she would have told him to come and sit by JD's bedside when she didn't even like him, but I didn't know for sure. I also didn't know that they used Robert's blood, but I did know that my blood didn't match my son's. *'Looks like I'm gonna have to get an investigator to investigate my doggone private investigator,'* I thought shaking my head.

"JD."

"Yeah dad?" he asked pausing in his routine to look at me.

"I love you son."

"I know," he replied turning away.

"I'll be back on Sunday; your Godfather will be here tomorrow okay?"

"Sure dad," he said then added quietly, "I love you too."

I left the rehab facility and called Janine immediately from the car, "Hey Neene, why is Rob sitting at our son's bedside?"

"What are you talking about Jon?" She said, I could just imagine her rolling her eyes as she said it.

"JD said that Robert has been at his bedside not really saying anything, just sitting there with him, keeping vigil like he has a right to be there."

"You might wanna ask him that yourself Jon. You invited him back into our lives by bringing him to the hospital with you when JD had the accident. Didn't he even donate blood, like someone asked him too? What the heck were y'all even doing together anyway?"

"Yeah, matter of fact he told JD that he was there to make sure that his blood didn't kill him," I replied avoiding her questions. I needed answers.

"What? Did they even use his blood?"

"I don't know. All I know is that they didn't or rather they couldn't use mine," I replied as I hung up.

I got home early and saw there was no one there, so I walked over to Marcus's house to pick up Amber, but Janine was already there chillin'. Amber was downstairs in the playroom with Myles and Monique, hanging out, watching Nick Jr., eating some popcorn and laughing out loud. It was good to see how tough our kids were. You wouldn't think that their mom was dying or that their brother had lost their limb. The adults in their lives were just barely holding it together or at least I was, but when I came back upstairs to the kitchen where they were, Marcus and Janine were laughing and Michelle was grinning hard too. Maybe it's just me feeling the crunch, but I didn't see anything funny.

"What's up guys? What's the joke? I need a laugh," I said.

"Hey bro," Marcus looked up at me, brows tight. "What's up? You alright?"

"Yeah, just needing a laugh," I smiled slightly. "What's so funny?"

"The kids were arguing about what channel to watch, you know Myles and Monique are a few years older but baby Amber was bossing them around something terrible! We were just laughing about how she was just like her momma – always thinking she's the boss of somebody, no matter how much bigger than her they are!"

I chuckled, "Yeah, that's Neene alright. Come on honey; get the kids. I'm ready to go. I had a long day. This commute every two days is really killing me."

"Wait! Tell us how JD was looking today babe," Janine said quickly, "I saw him yesterday and he was excited about his new robotic leg! It was hurting where they attached it for him when he was done working out, but he seemed so happy to be able to stand…"

"Well, I met his therapist today and that was cool, he has him doing some increasingly hard workouts, which I thought was great. And he told me that we have all the equipment we need too, which was a relief," I returned evenly.

"Really, what's his name?" Marcus asked flexing and checking out his bicep. "I need to get back into the gym myself."

"Kirk Jones," I replied to Marcus while watching Neene closely and saw she paled just a little. "Go get the baby Janine."

"Okay honey," She replied a little too eagerly. "Mishie, come with me downstairs just in case I need back up - That little Amber is something else!"

"She gets it from her mama!" Michelle replied laughing.

As Michelle and Neene walked downstairs laughing, I said to Marcus, "Why does the rehab dude from Prime Town Center Gym, look just like Robert? And another thing - Why the hell was Robert at my son's bedside, when Janine and I weren't there?"

Marcus' face said more than he would, "The therapist looks like Robert? Dude that's weird and I have no idea why Robert would be at JD's bedside man… Are you alright?"

"Nah man. Nah," I said as I walked back to my house alone.

CHAPTER 14
Robert: Plotting

I knew I had to do something, but what? I wasn't sure yet, but something had to be done. My son was about to be raised by a man I can't stand and my woman was willing to let me go just so that she didn't disrupt their life. I still don't get it. I can take care of my son and little Amber too.

I sat in JD's hospital room while he slept the other night, just watching his chest rise and fall. I wondered about all that I'd missed; his first steps, his first lay-up, talking to him about girls. I knew listening to Jon would lead him astray even though Jon seemed to be so high and mighty lately, being a Deacon and all. Underneath that façade, he was still a two-faced hypocrite and even more so now than before. How dare he pressure Janine to stay with him when we both know he has a whole 'nother family!

Jon had to pay, and after I show his ass this tape of Janine and I getting it in on my chrome desk, he'll be crushed enough to let this marriage to my woman go. Plus, once I show Janine the pictures of Leslie's son, it's a wrap for the two of them altogether. I stood up; feeling a lot better than I did when I sat down, checked my surveillance cameras for any activity in the parking lot and rolled out.

CHAPTER 15
Janine: Daddy's Baby

When I arrived to her office today, Dr. Latasha seemed to be determined about something. I knew it immediately because after the preliminary hellos, she was all business.

"Hmm… Ok. Let's switch gears for a brief moment Janine."

"Okay," I replied cautiously.

"Can you recall an example of a relationship that worked from your childhood?"

I paused for a moment taken aback a bit, after going through my mental Rolodex, I found myself coming up short and dismayed by what it may mean. "Actually, Dr. Williams – I can't. Most of my cousins and aunts are single, and the ones that are married don't seem to be enthusiastic about each other. Jon and I were the exception, even though I felt disconnected, maybe even from the beginning."

"Don't despair, many people cannot think of a good example, especially in their early family lives. There is more dysfunction in relationships as of late, than real relating going on, so don't feel upset about not having a touchstone. Tell me about a relationship that has influenced you and how you choose to relate with men instead."

"After a string of no-good boyfriends, my mom finally settled down with one guy and married my step-dad, but I knew he wasn't my real dad. The other men in my mother's life barely acknowledged my existence, much less told me I was pretty or smart."

"Tell me more about this time in your life."

"At first my mom tried to make up for my dad's leaving by working hard and being not only a successful paralegal, but thrifty when it came to spending as little money for the best NY had to offer us and not rely on any man for much. We shopped Macy's, Bergdorf's, Saks and Lord & Taylor's sale racks ever since I could remember; she showed me that you should always buy quality classic clothing – it never goes out of style and will last you a lifetime. She also exposed me to different cultures and foods with trips to Chinatown for dinner and movies with groceries from the markets there as well as midtown from Zabaar's and Citarella, but all of the fly clothes and cultural exposure didn't fill that feeling of something being missing."

"So…" Dr. Latasha dragged the word out softly then stated, "Are you telling me that clothes and exposure to different cultures was how you dealt with what you were feeling about your father? Or…" she left off leadingly.

"Yeah. I guess you could say that I dealt with missing my dad by buying mad fly clothes and with the love of Chinese and Japanese cultures. I even traveled to Japan with school my sophomore year, but all that… It never quite filled the void of wanting a man to treat me like I was his babygirl."

"Babygirl. Is that a term of endearment for you? Did your dad call you that as a young girl? Tell me more about that."

"Now that I think about it, my uncles and my daddy called me babygirl all my life. Well my dad did until he left, but even when I talked to him after we reconnected, he called me that. So have most of my boyfriends too. I don't know what it is doctor… I expect to be taken care of and people who will, show up and treat me like that – like their babygirl. It's not just men either. Older women at church call me babygirl too… Has no one ever called you that before?" I asked curiously. I mean if no one ever thought her to be precious enough to want to protect and love maybe she's got issues too.

"Well," Doctor Latasha countered looking me squarely in the face, "Personally, I feel like it's a cop out. An easy way to not use someone's name but make them feel special at the same time. I am not a baby, nor am I a girl. I am a grown woman and the only man I want to call me baby is my husband, and even then – only when it's appropriate. It makes me feel like someone is taking advantage of my womanhood or dismissing it completely for an idea of me that's unreal."

"So you think it's disrespectful?" I asked, astonished by her stance on something I thought was so benign.

"In a way, yes; I am a grown up; I have accomplished many things and although my dad still calls me his La-la from time to time when I need cheering up or in jest – it's not something I would hear anyone else being called, so maybe that's why I can't relate."

I sat there digesting what she said just mulling over in my mind why I loved to be considered "babygirl." I thought about how I actually was the baby girl in the scheme of my family tree, my mother was the baby girl, I was her oldest baby girl, and the last of the cousins from that generation. I had been "babygirl" all my life even without my daddy being there.

"What did you think about your parents' divorce?" Dr. Williams asked quietly breaking into thoughts of how much maybe being a "babygirl" was part of my overall problem.

"I was confused to be honest doctor. It made me wonder what I'd done to make my daddy leave at first, and then I began to think that maybe, just maybe it was me. Maybe he left my mother because of me. I made things change between them right? The waking up early to care for me, my mother's weight gain; maybe I made her lose interest in him. Or him in her."

Doctor Williams peered at me over her glasses and asked, "What about their process do you actually remember?"

"Not much doctor," I replied lying through my teeth. It was too traumatic to go into; the other woman, the screaming and fighting… I couldn't see why it mattered why or how they broke up. All that mattered was that they did.

"How about your process?"

"I don't know how I processed it. I think it was mostly shock, sadness and anger. I know now for sure that when he left, he took my blueprint. He was supposed to show me what to look for in a man, but he turned his back on me. Now that I think about it, I was just angry doctor. At both of them – Her for driving him away, him for letting her make him want to leave me, myself for making her stop loving him and not loving him enough!" I sat there and zoned out after that tirade, when I finally looked up into her face, she was watching me intently.

"You said you were angry with your mother for making him want to leave you. And you also said that you were mad at yourself for several reasons. Tell me what you remember about what happened when he left. I think we need to explore this before we go any further."

It took me a minute to get back to the place where it all fell apart for good with my parents. When I pulled up the memory in my mind, my eyes filled with tears; I could picture the kitchen curtains – red and white gingham and the sun shining in the windowpane, which belied the scene in front of me.

"My father grabbed my mother by the front of her shirt and was screaming in her face, 'Shut up! Dammit Jo! Shut up! It's not like that!' While she screamed back, 'You and that whore!' Then I remember him forcefully backing momma up against the kitchen counter. Momma was cryin', I was cryin' and even daddy was crying. She kept screaming, 'Leave and go wit' her ass then! Just leave! *Leave*! You bastard! I hate you so much!' He smacked her; she reached for the kitchen knife and sliced his hand as he tried to grab it from her. Then I started screaming, 'Please momma don't kill daddy. Please, please, please momma please...' Slowly, they both stopped and turned to look at me. My dad let go of my mom and picked me up, but I was so scared of him and the blood dripping from his hand, that I started to flail my arms at him, hitting him saying, 'Let me go! Let me go!' His whole face masked to a look I have never seen before or since, then he put me down, grabbed a bag he already had packed and left. I never saw him again as a child."

"I want to try a new technique with you called The Empty Chair. It's where you talk to the person you haven't had an opportunity to talk to, letting them know how you feel or what you think about their impact on your life. What do you think? Wanna try it?"

"Okay doc, I am game to do this, but what do I do exactly? Picture him as he was then? Because I have no idea what he would look like now," I replied.

"Yes, picture him as he was then and think of all the things you wanted to say to him as you were growing up. Use this as your chance to let him know how you felt and how he impacted your life then and now."

After a moment or two of imagining myself as a child and him back then, I replied, "Okay, I think I can do it Dr. Williams." I watched as the doctor rearranged the chairs in her office, so that there was a chair facing me and she sat down on the sidelines.

She explained to me, "Imagine you are your 10 year old self, think about your frame of mind, what you wore then, how you sounded, and even your hairstyle. Then visualize your dad sitting there and the same for him; his style, his facial expressions and tell him how he has hurt you with his absence. I will sit here as a silent observer and if you need to stop, you can at any time."

I felt kinda foolish, I must admit, but I thought it would feel good to finally get off my chest what I'd wanted to say since I was daddy's little girl.

I took a deep breath and faced the chair thinking about how my mother did my hair in pigtails and the way my daddy used to look at me when he came home from work – Like I was so beautiful and precious to him. Finally, I said, "Daddy, why did you leave? Why didn't you take me with you? What about me? I missed you so much on my birthdays and holidays and not for the gifts you used to give, but just for your being there, watching and smiling. I didn't have you to tell me about boys or to screen them out for me. You never showed me how a man treats a woman when times get rough. I cried at night wondering what I did to make you leave. You missing every major event in my life graduating from elementary and junior high school, high school and college, made every event seem less exciting and fun. I just kept thinking about you where you were, if you thought about me, if you had more children, if you missed me. I wanted to hate you Daddy! I wanted to make you feel how I did; alone, sad, angry, but I didn't know how to so…"

Dr. Williams allowed the silence to fill the room, then after a few minutes passed she said, "So… What Janine? What happened? How did you get back at your dad?"

I didn't answer right away, I couldn't. Tears were streaming from my eyes and all that kept cycling through my mind were the faces of men I had given my body and time to for money and affection with over the years; the older man from the club who reminded me of my father and treated me like his little prized possession, the drug dealing dude who wanted me for his trophy. Even Jon fit into this category. To him I felt like I was a trophy wife, little more than someone to make him look good, but not someone he shared himself with fully. It dawned on me that it was all for my father's love. All because I missed him… All because he decided to leave me behind without a road map of what to demand and expect from a man who wants to love me.

I let the silence swallow the room and sat there wallowing in the realization of my part in my own demise. I left her office without saying another word.

On the way to my next destination, it dawned on me that I was the Wayward Woman from Proverbs 2:16-19 we discussed in pre-marital counseling with Bishop. The woman who leaves destruction in her wake; my family and lovers all were bearing the brunt of my deception and the worse part about it is that I didn't even consider them in my decisions. When we did our counseling, he gave Jon this scripture and me Proverbs 31 to study, he told us that Proverbs 31 was for me to know exactly what I needed to be and Proverbs 2:16-19 were for Jon to know and understand what he didn't want to have. I remember it clearly because as soon as we left Bishop's office, we switched handouts and laughed, me because I was nervous about the implications and Jon because he was so sure he had what he read.

When Jon came upstairs after ripping my clothes off of me last night, he pulled out those scriptures from our family bible. He said that he knew I had been the wayward woman, but he also knew that the Proverbs 31 woman was inside me as well. He reminded me that our old man is an ever-present thorn in our sides, but we have to be strong and unwavering in our ability to choose to do what's right in the face of what's easy or what feels good for the moment. Then he told me that he knew I had been unfaithful to our marriage, but he had faith that I could choose to be a better wife. He just wanted to know if I wanted to be that wife. He couldn't go on not knowing if I loved him at all over the past 20 years of marriage and stay sane, much less married to me. But, when I asked him about Leslie and he said, "Leslie who?" I was done. He had the audacity to act like he didn't know what I was talking about. He must think he's exempt. Well, he's about to find out he's not.

CHAPTER 16

Janine: Christ's Living Well's Shelter

I was supposed to meet with Mishie for lunch after my session today, but she wasn't feeling well and said she wanted to reschedule for Friday. I made a mental note to stop by her house after work the next day, bring her some flowers and chat before my hair appointment. Plus, I wanted to check on the sitter we shared and my baby Amber. I arrived back at my job for the evening shift feeling lost; I wanted to disappear into the world of someone else's troubles.

Nikki, our shelter's intake specialist, was waiting for me and as soon as I walked in to my office, she came strolling in feigning nonchalance, "Hey Mrs. Dupont. How are you?" Before I could say anything, she continued, "I know I'm on the schedule tonight until 7, right – but I wanted to know if I could please leave early. I have to pick up my son from daycare, he's throwing up, so they won't keep him and there is no one else to pick him up."

At first, I was so taken off guard I just stared at her. I guess she began to feel uncomfortable, because she kept talking. "I know it's short notice, but I will make up the time if you need me to Sister Dupont." She pleaded.

I found my voice and had to apologize. "Of course, Nikki! Go get lil Carlton – I apologize for not answering right away. I was taken off guard a little bit with your timing; I'm here, but I haven't quite gotten settled yet." I said with a slight smile.

"I am so sorry! I wasn't even thinking…"

"No, no! Oh it's okay, I understand… When our children need us, nothing else matters." I said, slowly shaking my head, hoping the movement would stop the tears from falling from my eyes.

Nikki came around my desk and put her arm around me saying, "I know things are hard right now Sister Janine, but God has a way of showing up and showing out when you least expect it. Hold on to your faith." She gave me a squeeze said, "See you tomorrow," then with a small smile she stated, "and remember the mustard seed," as she walked out of my office.

If only she knew the truth. I wonder what she would think then. I looked at my desk and my eyes fell on the pictures of my children at various moments of their lives. Amber in diapers with her lopsided grin, then one with her taking her first teeter-tottering steps; JD as a little, big-headed, toddler laughing while sitting on Jon's shoulders and then another with him hitting a jump shot at last year's homecoming game, and I let the tears fall unchecked. I knew my mascara was running, but there was no stopping the torrential downpour of tears. I knew I had messed over all of our lives and all I could do was pray that God would intercede at some point, before it all ended in tragedy. I'd been operating outside of the will of God in most of my actions to date, but I wanted to change so I would be given some grace and mercy from what I saw coming for my family due to my careless behavior.

I sat at my desk and pulled out the journal Dr. Tasha had given me a few weeks ago to write a journal entry:

June 1

I know that I'm not as perfect as I appear to be at first glance, many of my church friends and co-workers look at me and think, 'Oh, Deacon Dupont's wife is so lucky, but little do they know how it feels to be me. Me, the one who is afraid of being alone in the dark. The one who's addicted to the touch of a man and up until now, that man wasn't her husband. Sister Jolene, that gossip mongering heifer, would have a field day if she knew what really went on behind the French doors she admires so much when she visits. Humph. It's wrong, but the thought of her being in shock, makes me a lil bit happier. The piety of the women in church is sometimes sickening. The only thing is, I just know that it would reflect poorly on our family and Jon especially. And my ministry is so integral to the community! I can't allow anything to make our good works be overshadowed by our human failings. I don't want to dishonor my husband's reputation in the church, but he has another woman in North Carolina! Who knows what he is doing with Leslie?! She is just a big-breasted version of me anyway. A cheap imitation. I remember when he dropped her and got with me. She was sick! She kept calling and calling to the point where Jon just gave me the phone. After I politely told her we were expecting and getting married at the end of the semester, she broke down crying and I never got word of her calling again… I was so hurt when Robert showed me those pictures. Jon never really gave her up after all of these years…

Initially, I wanted to confront him and make him pay for making a fool of me all of these years, then I realized that I felt the same way Jon would feel if he found out about Robert and I. And I knew I had to stop sleeping with Robert, but I was too weak to break it off. But, when I went to his office after being called in for an appointment, I wanted to know what he wanted with my family and why he was at the hospital with Jon when JD got hurt. He ignored my questions and told me he wanted me back. I told him I was done with cheating on my husband and I was going to tell Jon about us. He didn't believe me; he just grabbed my hair and shoved his tongue in my mouth! My tears and pleas went unheard. We grappled and argued for about 20 minutes with him trying to get under my skirt, fondle my breasts, bite and suck on me to the point where I couldn't fight anymore; my body and mind would not agree; the familiarity of his touch overwhelmed me and I just let him take me. I was done.

He bent me over the chrome and glass desk in his office and all I heard was him moaning gutturally with the intermitted grunt of - "I love you Janie." What could I do? Afterwards, I told him I would tell Jon that he raped me. I'd told him I didn't want to! I told him that I had changed and wasn't going to be that kind of woman anymore. He'd laughed at me and sneered, "What kind of woman Janie?" I told him I would report him to the police. He retorted he would tell Jon that we had been seeing each other in college and never stopped throughout my marriage to him, which wasn't altogether true, but it was true enough to tear my world apart by the seams.

As I wrote the last word, the intake buzzer started to ring. I quickly wiped my eyes, checked my make-up and went to the door. I saw a young woman standing there with two small children; she didn't appear to be over 19 years old, but the children, who looked like her mini-me's, were at most three or four years old. A disheveled mess, they looked as if they had traveled far by foot and public transportation. The plastic Kroger bags they carried were full of holes and over-flowing with clothing. The little dirty-faced angels – their gap toothed smiles caked up with Mc Donald's barbecue sauce, the streaks cracking on their cheeks with their happy meal toys clenched tightly in their fists as they held one another's hands tightly and peered up at me.

The young woman with them looked harried and stressed, her face tear streaked and make-up free. She asked, "Is this the chu'ch shelter?" As if she half expected to be turned away.

"Yes. Please come in, and let me take those bags for you. What's your name?" I smiled as I reached out and grabbed the bags she'd sat down on the pavement outside the large house to console the children. Women of the Well Shelter sat to the left of the Christ's Living Well's main building and served as the church's women's homeless shelter ministry and as a free daycare for the women and children of the church.

We only had the capacity for eight women and twelve children to live in the shelter at a time and provided them with counseling, food, shelter and access to Georgia state welfare and housing systems for free. This small group of vagabonds filled us to capacity.

It was partly my brain child and I wished I had more time to devote to it, but I'd decided when I had Jon Jr. that I would create a position for myself that would make it possible to work on being the best mother I could, while making sure that single mothers who struggled, would have a safe haven to help them get back on their feet.

I watched as the young woman pried the two small children apart and picked up the smaller little girl whispering, "We safe now babydoll. Don't worry, mamma's here." She grabbed the older boy's hand, turned to me in the foyer and said, "My name is Stacen, this here's my boy David and his baby sister name Star. We need somewhere to stay. My friend Malinda said that the shelter here at this church helped her get her own place; she said it was clean and you all was really nice. We just can't stay with my uncle no mo'. He just ain't right."

The way she said that last thing triggered something in me that I couldn't quite touch on, but knew right away what she meant by it. Her face suddenly appeared haunted, like a spirit passed before her eyes and then the expression was gone just as quickly. I almost thought I imagined it.

"Well," I said quietly, still studying her face for traces of the apparition, "don't worry about all of that now. Let Sister Angela take the children to the playroom to play, while you and I go back to my office, sit down and take care of the paperwork for your stay."

"How long can we stay here," she asked eyes wide, she took in the community room where the other young mothers were assembled, talking to one another and on the computers looking for employment as I led her through to get back to my office.

"The usual length of stay is about six-eight weeks. We are usually able to get our young women back on track, in more ways than one, by then." I sat at my desk and saw my open journal sitting there. I quickly put it into my desk and started a file for our new entry "Okay, Stacen my name is Mrs. Dupont, but many of the young women here call me Sister or Ms. Janine. I am going to ask you a few questions and I want you to answer as best you can. Is that okay with you?"

"Yes, Ma'am."

"Ms. or Sister Janine... You said that Malinda referred you to us. Is that Malinda Jackson?"

"Yes! You 'member her?"

"I sure do! I lead orientations every other day. How is Malinda doing?"

"She's doing just fine Ms. ..."

"Janine…" I prodded her along.

"Right. Ms. Janine," she repeated slowly, then added, "she just got a really good job down at'ah Kroger as a head cashier. She's been working there for a while… Since she left here with her certificate and got her a place of her own."

"Speaking of certificates, do you have the children's birth certificates with you?"

"Um... Yes, right here," she said pulling the documents from a worn manila envelope.

I took the documents from her and began to record hers and the children's full names and birth dates on the intake sheet; Star was two and David was three years old.

While I began to neatly print their names, I asked quietly, "Is there someone we can call in case of an emergency?" This question was hard to answer, but even harder for me to ask. Most of the women who come here are running from one situation or another, be it an abusive spouse, an irate parent who has lost all hope for their future or addiction that has rendered them homeless and unable to care for themselves and their children. Stacen on the other hand was a different case; she had been abused in a different way.

She was beautiful, long graceful neck, and hair braided into a heavy naturally curly braid over her shoulder. Her cocoa complexion was radiant despite her red, almond shaped eyes and tear-streaked face. Her figure did not reflect her having had two children either. She had on a brightly colored tight baby-tee that barely reached the waist band of her tight fitting jeans and a pair of Old Navy, 1.99 flip flops in bright orange with her pretty chocolate toes painted to match. She flipped her braid to her left shoulder and said quietly, "No Ma'am."

I inquired about the uncle as I had too, it was the last place she resided according to what she had murmured earlier, "What about your Uncle? What's his name and number?"

"If anything ever happens to me, I don't want him to know nothing! Especially about my babies," she stated emphatically, then looked to the floor unable to meet my eyes again.

"Okay, that leads me to my next question – Is there anyone that presents any harm to you and do they know that you have come here for shelter?"

"No, he 'on't know where I went. I ain't take no bags wit' me jus' plastic market bags I been saving, so he 'on't start lookin' for us 'til tomorrow, maybe."

"Okay, Stacen why did you leave where you lived? Was it unsafe and if so, in what way?"

"I ain't know you asked dese kinds of questions…"

"You don't have to answer if you feel uncomfortable, it will just assist us in getting you services…" I answered leaving her open to decline or answer the questions. We both knew there was something that she needed to reveal about her uncle and I think we both knew what that was.

"I guess… I wanna know who sees what I'm gonna tell you before I do." She hesitated.

"I understand that completely. It will be me, and the appropriate counselor who I refer you to for help. No one else, unless you would like for us to tell someone else…" I knew she was past the age for mandatory reporting of rape and/or molestation, but that all depended on when it started and if she was willing to go through the process. She would have to want to tell and perhaps even tell the story herself again and again, if she reported it.

The silence grew and stretched, hovering over our heads and seeping into our skin. It was heavy and thick like a heavy rain cloud waiting to burst open and shower us with acid rain in place of truth. I felt like she was attempting to make sense of the revelation to another person what she didn't really want to reveal to anyone.

"Ms. Janine…" She paused, took a deep breath, then said in a hushed voice… "My uncle is my kids' daddy. I told him I didn't want to do it no more. I was tired 'a him using me and hurting me… Ms. Janine, I was just so tired. I told 'im stop or I was gonna tell the police. He laughed at me and threatened to take my babies where I would never be able to find 'em. I was scared because I don't have folks, so I asked Malinda what she thought I could do and she told me to come here."

"You don't have folks…" I questioned, quietly shocked.

"No, ma'am. When my parents died in an accident on the highway, I went'ah live with my mother's sister and her husband. I's around 11 years old back then. My auntie died when I was 16 and my grandparents been dead a long time. So, no – I don't have no folks."

"How are old are you now, about 19 right?" I asked, looking at her unfinished chart. "When did the abuse start Stacen?"

"When I was about 12 he started touching me, my aunt was real sick and nobody knew why at first, but we found out it was cancer," her eyes welled up with tears and she began to whisper, "when I got about 15, he started to force me to do things to him, then one day after my auntie died, he just got on top of me…" She stopped talking and began to sob, tears rolling down her face and dripping from her chin.

I sat watching her cry for a moment just stunned, then finally gave her a box of tissues and let her cry for a few more minutes undisturbed. The betrayal of her trust struck me deeply, I recalled how I told about being touched by my cousin and the consequent dismissal by my family, but what if there were no one to tell, at all, ever? I began to understand right then, that I needed to talk to Dr. Tasha because she put things into perspective for me; she let me know that what happened to me was not my fault and that I should have been protected, but that I also had to let it go, forgive and love myself despite what had happened to me. I realized that for Stacen, leaving her uncle's house was the first step for her on that road and mine was deciding to go through with the therapy.

I continued to fill out her paperwork making sure to note that she had no family and no one was authorized to see her children. Then, I called Doreatha, our abuse counselor, to come in so that she would be able to meet with Stacen and schedule her first meeting right away.

I turned to Stacen, who was wiping her face and collecting herself and said maternally, "Ms. Doreatha, our in-house counselor, is coming to talk briefly with you right now and she will schedule some sessions with you while you stay with us. Is that okay with you?"

"Yes, I feel like I need to get this load off my back. I'm tired of carrying it! I knew it was wrong what we were doin', but he wouldn't stop - made me feel like it was my fault and I's just a lil' bitty thang when he started doin' that mess to me!" she said, her tear streaked face creased angrily.

"You have every right to be angry and upset Stacen." I said grabbing hold of her hands and looking into her face intently, and then added, "You also have to forgive and move on with your life so that you are able to raise those beautiful babies without anger and resentment in your heart – it's the only way."

I knew from experience, living life carrying a burden that way, leads to drama, pain and confusion for yourself and everyone you love. It made me want to bless God for the experience because if I hadn't had it, I wouldn't have had the wisdom I gained making to the other side to share with this young woman.

CHAPTER 17
Robert: Discovery

I watched Jon on my monitor, walking into my office with his head down. He looked like his heart was heavy and he didn't really want to know what he already knew; I knew the look. Many of my clients come in with that same look on their faces, fear etched into the corners of their eyes and mouths twisted into permanent frowns. I listened in and watched as my aunt greeted him appropriately this time.

"Hello Mr. Dupont." Aunt Aggie stated, coolly looking over her cat rimmed glasses.

"Hi Ms. Aggie."

"Mr. Matthews will be with you shortly. Is there anything I can get for you?" Aunt Aggie asked him, her cataract rimmed green eyes dared him to say yes.

I felt like I should send for him before Auntie got indignant, so I hit the buzzer interrupting his response, "Please send in my next client, Ms. Douglas."

"Yes sir."

I heard her say icily, "Mr. Matthews will see you now."

As Jon walked in, the rage I built up over the past 18 years threatened to come to the surface. I had to get up and get myself a glass of water from the glass decanter to squelch the fire I felt like spewing. I'd thought by this point I would've been able to claim his wife, my love, once and for all, but my victory was being stolen from me and I had to go with the flow instead of directing the course of action.

"Hi Jon. How are you?" I greeted him with a smile, choking back resentment and hatred.

"I don't know. You tell me. How am I? What do you have to tell me?"

"Well, I'd rather talk about some other things first, you know – the niceties." I forced myself to grin, "How's JD doing? How are things at home?"

"Actually, JD is doing much better... He mentioned that you were at the hospital when his mother and I weren't there. I don't recall you saying that would be part of your investigation though..."

"Oh, yeah," I cut in trying to minimize that whole discussion. I had to see my son. I knew it might be the only time I would be able to see him alone and look at him closely without scrutiny. I knew he was mine after my blood matched and Jon's didn't, which he didn't even know; it pays to have connections. "It was to see who else would be stopping by because of what you told me about the blood work. The incident was publicized so, I figured that the father might come to check on his son if he'd heard about it."

As Jon sat and pondered what I'd said, I thought back to the news reports on the accident. The reporters described Jon and Janine like celebrities, *'Atlanta architect and power broker, Jon Dupont and socialite wife Janine Dupont's son was crippled in a horrific car crash with a tractor trailer!'* Pictures of the wreckage from the accident and of them leaving and entering the hospital with Jon's arm around

Janine, shielding her from the cameras; her face covered in large black sunglasses. I came back to the present to look into my arch-enemy's face; he was broken, but angry by the looks of it and I was only going to make it worse, which gave me great pleasure.

"Well, Jon I have some things to tell you that may not be what you want to hear, but like most men or even women who come to me for this type of investigation, it's what you already know. Janine has been involved with her personal trainer, Kirk Jones for the past three months as far as we can tell. When did you notice that something was off?"

"Right around the time I came to you three months ago. I knew it had to be something." He shook his head dejectedly, "I just wanted to believe that everything was okay, but I knew it wasn't."

"So now what? Do you want me to gather the evidence for court proceedings?"

"…No, there won't be a divorce."

"Really? Why not? If you don't mind me asking…"

"Janine and I already talked about it and she didn't tell me who, but she confessed and I forgave her. The thing that's really bugging me is JD. I mean, who is his dad? I just don't understand," Jon ran his hand down his face frustrated.

"Maybe I can shed some light on *that* situation for you." I smiled slowly savoring lowering the boom on him.

"How? What do y…," realization crossed his face and I knew he finally understood what transpired almost nineteen years ago. While he was out sleeping with Leslie and getting her pregnant, Janine came to him carrying my son.

"It's funny how life is, isn't it Jon. I was in jail for seven years and you *never* came to check on me, send me a letter, card, note, anything. Maybe if you had, I may have gotten the chance to tell you about Janine and I being together before you married her. Marcus came to see me, he knew about Janine and me, but he didn't know about JD. It's strange that all this time she never told me. But then, she never told you either. You know, I had to come out of prison and start my whole life over from scratch. Decided to live in the shadows because the limelight was just a little too bright for me, especially since the woman I love left me for you."

Jon sat there staring at me, eyes glazed over and I could tell he was re-living the past nineteen years of his life; fact-checking and fitting the pieces of the puzzle together so he could see what I already knew. He jerked up out of his seat furious, "You bastard! All this time you were playing me! And I came to you for help. How could you? I gave your ass money to get revenge on me! I should whip your ass!"

"You can keep your money Jon. It's no good here anyway. I got what I want." I smirked as I tossed the DVD of me and Janine to him.

"What's this?" he stood up angrily and caught the disc.

"Good catch," I snorted. "It's something I think you might enjoy – a little piece of the action caught in this very room. Wanna watch it together? I could do with reliving it right now; I need me a lil piece of Janine."

"You mutherfucker!" Jon launched himself across my desk so fast, I couldn't believe it. His hands were around my throat as we both fell against the window behind my chair. He kept saying, "You mutherfucker! You mutherfucker!" as he banged my head against the window and punched me in the face repeatedly. His weight was giving him the advantage because I was upside down with my legs in the air and trapped in my chair, but when he paused slightly to breathe, I took my chance and easily flipped him back over my desk sending all of my papers flying around the office, with him landing on the floor by the door.

"Call the police and Channel 46 news Aunt Aggie." I choked out as she walked in scared a moment later, surveying the damage. My office looked like a war zone. There was blood on the wall behind my desk, everything that at one time lived on my desk, found homes in various odd places; the glass and chrome lamp was upside down, smashed almost inside out. The chrome paperweight Neene had given me for my birthday was in a corner. The files I was looking at before his appointment, were splayed open, their contents mixed and tossed about like trash.

"I already did. They should be here any moment. Are you alright nephew?" Concern creased her forehead.

"I will be soon," I replied as I looked at Jon crumpled on the floor crying like a bitch. "He thought he was Hercules for a minute there Auntie, but he never could take me."

"I know Bobbie, I know. The police should be here any minute. Are you sure you don't need me t'a do anything else honey?"

"Nope." I replied as the officers arrived. They buzzed at the entrance and I let them in as Aunt Aggie went out to meet them.

"He's in there on the floor," Auntie Aggie said. Then added, "Yes, we will be pressing charges officer, he went plum mad in there!"

Satisfied, I watched them drag him out of the building handcuffed with the paparazzi snapping pictures. Now, he knew how it felt to be humiliated and have his heart ripped out on camera.

CHAPTER 18
Jon: Truth Telling Freedom

This mutherfucker! I can't believe this mutherfucker is the father of my son! Was all that ran through my head until he dropped the next bomb – *He had my wife on tape!* I lost it and lunged over the desk, murder in my veins and even as I sit here in this cold cell, I still want his ass dead.

The police were gonna let me go at first; on the way to the elevator, one of them said, "Look, if we let you go, will you just go home? We pick up angry guys from this location all the time, but they usually just need to blow off some steam. Will you walk it off if we let you go?"

I didn't respond, just struggled and strained against them and my restraints like a wild beast. I pushed one officer to the ground and tried to get back to that office to wrap my hands around Robert's neck again, but the other officer whacked me in the head with the Billy club. I fell to my knees.

"I guess this one's really angry," the one that hit me chuckled, like it was funny, "let me go see if the owner wants to press charges. You got him?"

"Yeah, I think he's gonna behave on the way down. Right buddy?"

"I'm good."

The other officer went to talk to Robert while we waited in the foyer for the elevator. He returned with a puzzled look on his face, "I don't know what this one found out, but the owner's gonna press charges looking at that office." He said to his partner. Then turned to me and asked, "Was it worth it?"

"Yup."

When they shoved me into the back of the squad car, it was surreal. The flashing lights and reporters roaring questions made me feel deaf and blind. Once on the ride to the station, the scene outside my car window ran together and didn't make sense; the sun shone red and sky was purple, but the ride was still too short to process any of it. I kept re-living the moment he sneered at me and said, *"Maybe I can shed some light on that situation for you."* Not only did I find out who my son's biological dad was, I found out that my wife and my ex-best friend had been playing me for the past 19 years. The question becomes, what now?

I got my one phone call before they processed me and called Marcus, but he was busy and didn't answer. I'd forgotten we had a client in town today for a job in South Carolina and I was supposed to be there myself. I know he was doing a great job covering for me though. I left a brief message; I need to look in his face when I ask him what he knows about Janine and Robert anyway. There was only one person left to call: her.

"Marcus called me a little while ago looking for you. Where are you? Jon – What's wrong?"

"I'm in county, need you to come bail me out."

"What! You're where? What in the world is going on with you? What happened?"

144

"Robert and I got into it at his office. Talk to you when I see you. I need you to get 100 thousand from the business account for them to release me. Please be quick about it."

She paused so long before responding I thought she'd hung up, and then she said, "I can explain."

"Oh, you will." I replied, as I hung up. I sat there fuming until they called me for fingerprinting and a cop escorted me to another room to take my prints.

"Weren't you just in the news for your son a couple weeks ago?

"Yes," I whispered, disgusted that he would recognize me based on the son that isn't even mine.

"Man look - I'm sorry this had to happen to you, most guys just take a walk and cool off. Why didn't you take the out?"

"You wouldn't understand, because you don't know what that man did to me."

"Well, it must have been something crazy by the look of him and his office." He gave me a side look and said, "He actually laughed when I went in there to ask him if he wanted to press charges, his head was bleeding all down his face and he just laughed this crazy laugh." The officer shook his head and added, "Just crazy."

"Yeah he is crazy. But he doesn't know just how crazy I am."

"Well, don't go getting yourself into more trouble, it's not worth it. You have a wonderful wife and family; don't ruin it because of him being a jack's behind." He said as he rubbed my finger onto the clear glass screen. I watched my print pop up on the computer monitor amused that he thought my wife was wonderful – that whore. I don't even know if any of my children are mine - *What family?*

He took me to a cell that was bare and cold after removing my belt and shoelaces and placing them into a plastic bag with my booking number: 0897311 written on it black Sharpie. The concrete floor was painted a slate grey and the solitary cot felt like slab of solid concrete help up by wire rubber bands. The door's loud series of clicks behind him had me shook. I didn't want to be there, I just wanted my self-respect and dignity back from the floor of Robert's office, but I had no idea how to go about getting it.

After about three hours, I heard voices behind the door. I thought I might be going a little crazy to be honest. I was in there praying non-stop for God to stop the thoughts of revenge that kept racing through my mind, because all I could see was blood on my hands and I wasn't sure whose it would be. I was still on my knees when they opened the door; all I saw was Janine's face, she looked tired – aged around her mouth and eyes somehow from this morning when I got out of bed from making love to her.

I looked at Janine, then said to the officer, "Can I have a minute alone with my wife?"

The officer replied, "No sir, you both have to vacate the premises at this time."

I didn't reply, I just allowed them to lead me out of the cell. The officer removed my shackles, had me sign some release papers and then brought me my baggie of belongings. Initially, I was quiet on the way to the car, but I had to say something. "Janine?"

"Yes Jon."

I opened the door for her and went around the car, collecting my scattered marbles. I sat in the driver's seat, slowly pulled out of the police station parking lot and said, "I need to know what's going on; I am on the verge of being back in prison forever if I can't bring some reconciliation between what's going on in my mind and reality. I want to trust you to tell me the truth at this point but simultaneously, I am wondering if you ever have."

"I won't lie to you again Jon. What do you want to know?"

146

"First off, I want you to know that I sat in that cell, praying for God to take the murderous thoughts away from me because, honestly, I want to kill you both."

Janine's eyes widened slightly, so I knew that what I'd said registered. "What I have to say won't be easy to digest, I know; but I hope that you would consider the good I have contributed to our lives – Jon, think of Amber."

"I am and I'm wondering if she's mine either."

"I believe Amber is yours, but let's start from the beginning."

"Believe?" I stopped myself from losing it, took a deep breath, and then continued. "Okay, what exactly is the beginning?"

"The night we all met at Club 112. I couldn't choose between the both of you. It seemed like you were in the lead at first, but Robert just kept staring at me and to be honest he was more my type at the time."

"We had a bet about who would be able to get you. I thought I had, but then you disappeared."

"What! A bet?" Neene stopped talking and just stared at me for a few seconds, before continuing. "Yes, I disappeared because Robert came to my house that night and we were inseparable for about 3 months, that is until his girlfriend met me at his house one day and we both broke up with him."

Things began to make sense all of sudden, Robert and I were just talking about this – I sent his woman to his house that day! So, all this time he was out for revenge? He had won the bet and never bothered to tell me or break up with his girlfriend properly and all the while I was screwing Leslie and like three other girls on campus thinking everything was cool! All I could do was shake my head at all of our lies and half-truths. "Okay, so at what point did you know you were pregnant?"

"I found out when I was just about 3 months. We had been together for about 3 months and you had already popped the question. There was no way I could tell you or him! Mishie kept telling me to, but I just prayed that he would look like you and everything would be okay. And for a while, a good long while, everything was…"

"Did you ever love me Janine or was I second best to Robert all of these years?"

"I did love you… I loved you then. I love you now."

"Were you sleeping with him after we were married Janine?"

"Yes, I did, but not immediately. It's only been in the last 5 years of our marriage after he was released from prison. I was really feeling neglected with you being away so much but, I really want you to know that I won't ever put out marriage in harm's way again."

I pulled the car over to the side of I285 with a peeling of tires and the acrid burning smell of scorched rubber filled the car. As it came to a full stop, I was already out of my seatbelt with my hand around Janine's throat. I didn't mean to kill her just to let her know how it felt to have all of the wind taken from you without warning and without mercy by someone you loved.

"Put our marriage in harm's way, *again*?" I said, as I watched her eyes bulge out of her head and fill with tears, her mouth open without sound. "What can you say that will make me stop choking you?" Her hands clawed at my wrists as she fought for her life. Slowly, I let go. I didn't want to really kill her, but I did want her to see how I felt on the inside. I was dying. Slow.

"There's nothing I can say Jon." She managed to get out, her voice sandpaper on wood.

"Well," I laughed, "there's something I want to tell you too."

"Okay," Janine said, tears standing in the corner of her eyes. I could tell she was breathing shallow – afraid. As well she should be.

"Leslie and I have a son a little older than JD." I said then turned to watch her reaction; she didn't disappoint. Her eyes widened slightly and the tears I wanted to see were released, leaving a black trail on her cheeks. Janine's face turned red then it began to twist into an angry grimace, but she seemed to remember what just occurred and slowly the frown began to relax and her eyes got a faraway look to them.

"I really wanted to tell you, but I just couldn't. My son, Jacob, was having a lot of issues in school, so I had to take more time out to be with him over the past few years." I added shrugging, twirling the knife.

"I already knew you were still with Leslie, splitting time between us; but I didn't know she had a son with you, but it makes sense. Now what? Am I gonna die today Jon? We've obviously never been faithful to each other, are we gonna start now or are we gonna let this go? Honestly, I don't want to let it go. I want my family."

"*Family*? Why does Robert have a video of you? Tell me that Janine - you act like it's all so cut and dry! You had sex with this man in his office! You can't be serious."

"He raped me."

"What?" I couldn't hear her; she was speaking so damn low.

"He raped me! He forced himself on me when I went to his office to tell him to back off and leave us alone. I told him that I chose you and he went off on me. Did you get the video? Did you watch all of that happen?" She said tears flooding her eyes again as she stared at me accusingly.

"He raped you?" I was stunned. "I tried to kill him when he said that he'd been with you and threw that disc at me, now I wish I had."

"I fought him off for as long as I could, but he bent me over his desk while I cried. I went past the gym and showered before I came home."

"What night was that? When did he do this to you?"

"The night before last."

That was it for me. I broke down and cried, this man abused my friendship and my wife; then when she came home, where there was supposed to be love and affection, I abused her as well. I drove home slow trying to think about my next steps, but so enraged I couldn't come to any conclusions. What was I supposed to do now? Kill him. How can I do that without going to jail when he's already set me up? Neene was silent next to me, but I could feel her eyes; fear and apprehension washed over me in waves. "He's gonna pay Neene. Don't worry."

"No, Jon. Just let it lie. Let it go."

"Let it go? Are you kidding me?" My voice filled the car as we veered off of our exit. "Insult added to injury and you want me to let it go?" I couldn't believe her!

"It's my fault. I shouldn't have gone to his office at all. I was just trying to avoid any more drama. I should have just come to you and confessed instead of going to tell him I was."

"Yes, it is your fault for being there, but it's not like you could have stopped him from taking what he thought was his Neene, trust me I know." Ashamed, I thought back to how easily he tossed me over his desk and on to the floor of his office. "But don't worry, he won't be able to use you against us anymore."

CHAPTER 19
Robert: The Sweetest Thing

I sat at my desk and laughed as those cops dragged his ass up outta here! I'm hoping the charges stick for at least a minute, so I can get close enough to my son to tell him who his real daddy is. Holding back has been killing me. I only stopped myself from telling him on the strength of Neene, but since she feels like Jon is the better option and choosing "her family" is more important, I figure she could have one less member and I can have a family of my own out of the deal.

My office phone rang loudly, and I thought Auntie was gonna get it but I guess she went to the bathroom, because it hang up and started ringing again. I checked the caller ID and saw it was Money, one of my investigators in the field on another case, but I could use him right about now for another mission.

"Hey, Money…"

"What up boss?"

"Go stake out University Hospital and text me when my client's wife, Janine Dupont, leaves."

"Aight boss. Do you want me to tail her too?"

"Nah, leave that to me."

"'Kay. Let me know if you need anything else. I'll be back on the stake out for the inheritance case."

"Cool."

As I hung up, I couldn't help but wonder why I was devoting so much time and attention to a woman who clearly didn't want me. I honestly couldn't figure it out. I didn't even want her ass no mo' to be real about it. I did want my son though. I wanted to be able to show him how a real man lived and grow him up right. His play-daddy was a punk. The worst kind too, the kind that had double standards. He wanted Neene to be the perfect picture, but he was never clean hisself. How you do that?

I never was an angel, but I never kissed and told until just now. I played around a lot as a youngin' but playing with Neene's heart was the first and last time I did a woman like that. Usually, I was upfront; I let the chicks know from the door, "Look this is gonna be a night to night type a' deal. Today it's you; tomorrow it could be your friend. What you wanna do?" All that money I had, them chicks were more than willing to share and not make too much of a fuss... Well, usually. I had to laugh at myself. I poured myself a shot of scotch and sat looking out at the city waiting for the next step to be made apparent.

"Buzz...," the text from one of my investigators read, "She just left."

I jumped in my jeep and headed to the University Hospital to see my son.

I arrived and slipped the pretty little nurse a crispy Benjamin. She said, "You don't have to do that Robert. You know I would do anything for you – plus I was here when you all got here together and you donated blood!"

152

"Thanks babygirl." I smiled at her pimping my dimples and started towards JD's room.

"He's asleep, let him rest Robert – he's had a long day today."

"I just came to sit and watch over him." I tossed over my shoulder as I entered his room.

I sat in the chair on the far side of the room and just watched his chest rise and fall. I couldn't believe I missed so much of his trials and errors. The walking and talking. The baby fat of him. The toddler laughs and giggles. The smell of breast milk and baby powder on his skin and in the chubby rolls of his neck. Now, he's been amputated. And I am pretty sure it was because he saw something he shouldn't have. The beeping of the monitors was starting to irk me. I guess they were irking him too because he started to stir.

"Dad?"

Damn. "Nah, it's me, Uncle Rob. You aight there son?"

"I'm thirsty Uncle Rob…"

I got up and poured him some water out of the little yellow pitcher on his side table and handed it to him as he slowly sat up a bit. "Here you go. How you feeling?"

"I 'on't know. Weird… Where's my dad? My mom was here earlier…"

"Not sure JD." I replied hoping he wasn't going to turn on the TV on one hand and hoping he would on the other. Maybe after I was gone, then I wouldn't have to witness him seeing it was me who had his father arrested.

"You and my dad were close weren't you? Is that why you're here sometimes?"

"Yes. We were best friends, but we grew apart. Now we…"

"I wonder if my friends will still be my friends now."

"Don't worry about the ones who leave because you have an obstacle to overcome. They were really never

153

your friends to begin with. You'll be better off without them anyhow. And you never know, maybe they will come around one day, when you're famous."

"I don't think I'mma be famous no more Uncle Rob," he said, voice cracking and eyes filling with tears.

"Only if you don't want to be. I ain't gonna say it's gonna be easy JD, not as easy as it has been for you so far, but the only one standing in your way is you."

"C'mon man. I only got one foot! Ain't no way…"

"Did you watch the Special Olympics this summer?"

"Don't nobody watch the *Special* Olympics Uncle Rob!" he replied rolling his eyes at me then giving me serious side-eye.

"Well in the special ones there are people who can out play those fools in the regular one! Don't doubt yourself. You gonna get therapy and as long as you work hard, your days as a star are still to come. I promise you."

"What do you know anyway? You don't play sports."

All I could do was laugh at first, then I replied, "Boy, I played in the NFL before you were born and when you were a little kid."

"What happened?" he replied eyes wide waiting for me to reveal how I came to be sitting here in his hospital room in a three-piece suit.

"A lot. A lot of stuff happened. I was stupid and I got cut because my ego was too big." And my heart was too broken to enjoy the fame.

CHAPTER 20
Janine: The Healing

I dried my tears and rubbed my bruised neck while I listened to Jon sob, and thought back to that moment in the salon a few hours before. I was in shock and called Mishie immediately after I got the call from Jon.

***

Initially, I sat at in the salon chair in silence while Jon tersely told me he was in County after he and Robert got into it at Robert's office! All I could say was, "I can explain." But could I really? I'm going to have to lay it all out on the line and I don't even know if I can. Am I even built for this kind of truth-telling?

When he hung up on me, I abruptly got up out of the chair with half my hair flat-ironed and half still kinky curly, and walked towards the bathroom.

My stylist, said, "Neene, everything okay?"

Instead of answering her I said, "Can you do the rest real quick when I come back from the bathroom? Straight is fine, I don't need curls today."

"Sure, no problem. You're okay, right?"

"Not exactly," I said without turning around as my iPhone dialed Mishie.

She picked up on the second ring, "Hey. What's up?" she croaked, voice rough and full of drug induced sleep.

"Ummm, have you heard anything from Marcus today?" I asked, hesitant to burden her with my ever-unraveling mess.

"Only that he just got a message from Jon about being in County when he was supposed to be at an important meeting." Fully awake now, she replied with a certain edge to her voice, "What the hell is going on Neene?"

"I'm in the bathroom at Kina's. I just got off the phone with Jon. Apparently Robert had Jon arrested after they got into it at his office."

"Did you tell Jon he raped you?"

"No. I couldn't. Mishie come on, how do you say that to your husband without expecting all hell to break loose?"

"Well, it looks like it may have anyway."

There was nothing I could say. She was right. I sat on the ottoman in the lounge area of the restroom peering into the gilded mirrors surrounding me, but not seeing them, or myself. I thought about how I could have fought back harder against Robert, although I was sure the tape he had showed me fighting him back and being overcome easily.

"Go get your husband Neene and tell him everything. It's time that he knew it all, even the parts he won't want to hear and you really don't want to tell. I'm sure he has some things he needs to let you know as well."

***

I really thought he was going to choke me to death when he had his hands around my throat in that vice grip. It was obvious, in retrospect, that we both have

156

been only fooling ourselves. Dr. Williams was right; I really needed to just make a decision as to what I really wanted and stick to it. So, I decided that I want Jon and my family. The thing is, does he still want me?

As he eased back into traffic headed home, I thought about bringing the joint sessions back up to him, but honestly, I was afraid. Afraid he might dismiss the idea. Afraid that he would want a divorce after all he knew. Simply afraid of what was next from this new, on-the-edge Jon.

After we had been driving a while he said, "Neene."

"Yes..."

"I'm going to make us an appointment to have a sit down with Bishop. I admit we need help to hash all of this out, but it needs to be with someone who has known us from the beginning and can bring God back into our marriage."

I said nothing. What was there to say? He was right and I guess that time in jail allowed him to think about more than just killing me.

We arrived to an empty house. Amber was at Mishie's helping her kids have a sense of normalcy, so there was no escaping what had just occurred between us. Surprisingly, the loss of pretense freed me. There were no more lies between us; he knew everything and so did I. I waited to feel anger or betrayal creep into my heart, but it never came. I don't know if it was because of my own dirt or because I had forgiven him in the hopes that he would forgive me, although I didn't expect it. Honestly, I was ready to face whatever would come of where we were. Being free made me understand that no matter what happened, if God would allow me to still be here, then it would all work out.

"So, what now, Jon?" I asked standing in front of him in the now infamous easy chair; things seemed so different from the last time we were in this position. For one, he was sober, and now, I was no longer guilty.

He looked up from thoughts. "I am going to take a shower, a long hot one. Then I'm going to call Bishop and have a long talk with him. What are you going to do?"

"I'm going to pray."

"What for?"

"For us, for our children, for our hearts to be made whole again, for strength to praise and worship God for allowing us to make it this far with all that's happened between us. I have a lot to pray for."

"You're right. You do have a lot to pray for. Make sure you pray for yourself too, maybe for clarity about what you really want from me and this relationship."

"I'm clear about that one, Jon. I want you and my family."

"Well, then maybe it's me who needs to be clear," he replied as he walked up the stairs to our suite.

I stood in the living room for a long while after he left. I stood and stared at the floor, where just two nights before he'd forced me to make love to him. I was only reluctant to make love to my husband because his ex-best-friend, my ex-lover, took me by force hours before; I wanted my husband then and I want him now. I really wanted to pray, but my mind was vacant. I just hoped He could hear my unspoken needs and would help me get back on His path for my life.

I ascended the stairs slowly, every creak of the stairs magnified by my creeping. I heard the shower running, knew he was in there by the way it sounded and decided I would join him. "*Why not?*" I thought. "*If he hates me, he'll put me out of the shower or be disgusted enough by my audacity and I will know what's up. If he doesn't put me out, then maybe we have a chance and can start the healing right away.*"

I cracked the bathroom door and saw him in the shower stall with his eyes closed, the water cascading over his chocolate bald head and down his back, his hands on the stone shower wall, facing the spray. I wanted in. I didn't even care that I had just gotten my hair done. I stripped down, crept quietly into the bathroom, cracked the shower door and slid in. Pressing my breasts against his back, I laid my head on his shoulder and let the water spray my face. I wrapped my arms around his belly and slid one hand to his dick, it stiffened and swelled in my hand, so I ran my hand along the underside and gripped the tip as I stroked him. He changed the water spray in the shower so that the showerheads that surrounded us hit us with intermittent bursts of piping hot water, shook off my embrace and turned around to face me.

"What Neene? You want me to make love to you like none of this happened?"

"No. I want you to make love to me like it did."

He grabbed my hair with one hand and forcefully turned me around in the shower, bending and penetrating me simultaneously. My face pressed into the stone as he began to grind himself into me, using my hair to bring me upright again for his assault. He rode me roughshod, one hand on my waist and the other one full of my breast, nipple wrenched between his fingers. We came hard and fast, leaning on me, his chest my shelter from the hot shower spray, my legs began to spasm and I turned, sliding my behind onto the built in bench. He hovered above me, seemingly searching my face, then turned to wash, leaving me sitting there spent.

"So... now what?" he said facing the spray.

"I don't know Jon. I just..."

"Neene, I really just need time to process all of this, I can't describe how I feel right now... Look, I know I love you, but I don't know what to think or feel about *us* right now. I need time and space." His shoulders shook as he said this and I wanted to reach out and hold him, but I didn't want to intrude on his space again so soon.

"Okay..." It was all I could say. It was easy for me, the obvious transgressor, to move on from what had happened, I suppose. But at the same time, what about his part in all of this? His being away from home? His other family in South Carolina? I was willing to forgive and move on, but would he be able to? Did he want to separate? All I had was questions. I rinsed off and got out of the shower, then went into my dressing room to blow dry my hair. I couldn't very well go back to the hairdresser again today, so I decided to smooth my hair back into a fluffy pony, throw on a track suit and go see JD, but I wanted to clear my mind before I went over there. I was feeling claustrophobic all of a sudden.

I turned on the radio and immediately heard my Bishop's voice! I will admit part of me just didn't want to hear any Word at the time. I kinda just wanted to wallow in my self-pity, but the whole point of not going straight to the hospital was to clear my mind and the Word has a way of making things crystal clear – even when you don't want to see it.

I began to follow as Bishop read this part of the scripture, "As she breathed her last – for she was dying – she named her son Ben-Oni. But his father named him Benjamin. So Rachel died and was buried on the way to Ephrath (that is Bethlehem). Genesis 35:18 &19.

When Bishop dropped the title of the sermon, I almost swerved! Unfulfilled Relationships. *Wow.*

"The power of contentment is being lost among Christians. Being fulfilled is having your needs, wishes and wants met, but at some level – in discontentment, you are saying that God is not on His job. Most people are living unfulfilled lives in their connections at work, in their personal lives and yes – even in their marriages."

I had to pull over. I parked the car on the street not too far from our alcove and settled down to listen to this entire sermon.

"People attempt to then gain fulfillment from the wrong things, clothes, drugs, people other than those they are committed to… It seems there is too much "self" taking precedence in their lives. No one is ever satisfied with anything anymore; the more they want, the less they take stock of what they have that is already working. They will take that *one thing* that isn't working and run into the ground…"

At that moment, I felt like all of my business was in the street. If Bishop knew, that means leadership at my church knew and that means my reputation was done. My mind started spinning with the possibilities of what may be happening amongst my peers if they knew all of my dirt but maybe, just maybe the enemy was trying to take my mind off of the matter at hand though… I decided to get focused, instead of getting paranoid.

"…We are always looking for what we don't have instead of appreciating what we do have. Focus on what is good and working and not what's not working… Rachel isn't happy with being the beloved and doted on wife, she wanted it all including what Leah had – children. She even tries in the chapters previous to this to make the issue of her closed womb Jacob's to fix! He had to tell her, you have to go to God to fix that! I can't. We go around expecting the people we are in relationships to fix things that only God can. God never promised you happiness. He promised you joy. Happiness means your outward expectations are met, but if they aren't you should be able to hold on to your joy."

Tears filled my eyes as I realized that I was missing that. Mishie had it. Marcus had been away the same amount of time that Jon had, but Mishie was content. She had her joy. It wasn't tied to Marcus particularly although she loved him dearly and was committed to their relationship. Her joy and her happy weren't tied together; mine was all wrapped up in Jon's presence instead of the presence of God and happiness with what I already had.

But Bishop was just getting started, "Rachel is a dissatisfied woman, although the plan was God's! Her attitude and character wouldn't facilitate what she wanted. She was the more beautiful of the sisters; the one Jacob worked 14 years for, the one that was used to getting and being the center of attention, she wasn't even a believer –

but Leah, she wasn't beautiful, she was older, and she was resigned to being second place to her sister but she also realized by the time she had Judah, that she couldn't keep tying her happiness to a man! She named all of her other sons' in reference to her desire for her husband, but Judah she named for her desire for God!"

I was Rachel. Lock, stock and barrel. I was the one who always had to have the attention. The adoration. Even amongst my friends. Everywhere. It was the reason I couldn't be alone and it stemmed from my need for my father as I found out in counseling, but it was even deeper than that. I needed to trust God's plan for my life and not continue to block my blessings like Rachel in an attempt to not only always get my way, but also in never being content with what God has already done for me! The tears were running down my face at this point. Makeup gone. Mind blown.

"Rachel had to die. She had to because she wasn't grateful. She was being competitive with her sister and couldn't deal with never being satisfied. Deal with that spirit of Rachel people of God. Kill her spirit within you now! This spirit is not a female spirit but the spirit of dissatisfaction and discontent that will lead you astray and make God feel as if you aren't worthy of the life He's afforded you thus far!"

By this time, I'm sitting in my car crying, snot running into my mouth and from my lips, all I can sob in prayer is, "Thank you Lord! Thank you for all that I have. Please Lord don't take it all away because of my spoiled, selfish ways. Kill that Rachel spirit within me Lord! Please Lord have mercy on me. Mercy Lord, mercy..." I sat for a minute in my car to blow my nose, wipe my face and gathered myself to go see my son.

I arrived at the hospital at nightfall. I planned on coming earlier in the day, but when Jon was arrested, it threw my visit time off. JD was usually asleep by now with all the meds they had him on, but I couldn't rest until I saw his face and kissed him goodnight.

"Hello Mrs. Dupont," the pretty, heavy-set nurse said as I approached the desk.

"Hey Nikki, is he asleep?"

"Yes ma'am. Go on in, I think he was asking about you earlier…"

"Thanks," I replied as I stepped into his cool, dark room. It was tomb still, but his soft breaths and the rise and fall of his chest reassured me.

The, "Beep… Beep…" of the monitors gave me comfort that all was as well as it could be in that moment. I stood over him taking in his curly hair, a mop at this point, no trace of a shape up remained. It somehow made him seem younger. His face relaxed in slumber made me want to return to the days when he was a stumbling toddler with a grubby face and a mop of curls just like this. I bent down kissed his face and ran my fingers through his hair.

"Mommy loves you JD baby," I murmured into his hairline.

"Mama…" he said rustling the sheets eyes still closed.

I stood watch over him until I was satisfied he was back soundly asleep then headed to Mishie's. I couldn't take being around Jon just then.

CHAPTER 21

Janine: Dealing Adult-like

"Hey girl." Mishie said answering the door in purple satin pajamas. She looked frailer than ever. "The nanny took all the children to the movies so I could rest. What's up?"

"Nothing, just came to check on you, see how you're feeling."

"I'm okay today, I wish I would go into remission though, I can't lie," she chuckled and walked slowly toward her favorite purple room. "How's Jon taking everything?"

"As well as could be expected, I guess. We're going to get some couples' therapy with Bishop."

"I'm glad. You guys need it to move past all of this, I think. People always acting like they don't need to talk things out, but we all do... I'm dying Neene."

"Don't say that Mish... C'mon... Don't... You can beat this thing. Remember your last track meet in college? You had broken your ankle the summer before and had to take the whole fall semester off. Then on top of that, you had to go up against one of our own to win the state championship! You not only did it Mishie, you dusted that Jamaican chick. She thought she was all that, you showed her..."

Mishie just looked at me blankly, seemingly resigning herself to my inability to cope with both of our problems at the same time. She closed her eyes briefly; sighed and then said, "Show me Neene. Show me that you and Jon can be fit Godparents for my children. Show me that you can show our children what it looks like to face heartache and heartbreak, but keep your family together. We don't see enough of that these days."

"I know, Mishie. I will do my best." Tears stood out in my eyes. I knew exactly what she was saying. '*I'm dying and I need you two to stay together for me and my family. Don't let your marriage fail.*'

"I've loved Marcus since that first time we saw them in the club that night, always, never wavering in my affection or commitment to the process of our marriage. That's how I am. My loyalty to you has never wavered, either right?"

"No," I replied staring intently at the violet shag rug beneath my feet. Where was she going with this?

"I need you to woman up. Make a decision, stick with it and deal with the consequences, like life in New York taught us to. You have to not only be a role model for Amber, but for my baby Monique and the women at the church and at the shelter who admire and respect you..." She paused and closed her eyes briefly her lips moving without words, as if in prayer, then said, "I know I didn't go as much as I should have... But I want you to make sure that Bishop Brown does my funeral."

"We are *not* about to start making funeral arrangements up in here! Mishie come on!" I paused, thinking of something to say to lighten the mood. "You have to be going into remission soon, I know it." But even as the words left my mouth and hung in the air between us, they rang hollow. She was dying. We both knew it.

"Well…" she paused, and then asked quietly, "What are you going to do?"

"I don't know." I sat back in the overstuffed, deep purple velvet chair next to her on the chaise lounge and looked up at the ceiling. I didn't know what to do. I was out of schemes and at this point just wanted to go with whatever Jon decided. I was okay with however it went until Mishie said all of this. "We're going to go into therapy, but there's always a chance that won't go the way we expect."

"Don't you have to finish up with your own therapist before you start with another one anyway?"

"Yes. I have to call Dr. Williams and make my last appointment."

"Yeah… I am going to need to have the kids and Marcus talk to someone when I'm gone. The hospital will set it up for me though."

"Have you talked to the kids about it yet?"

"I tried to break it down for them, but I can tell they know I'm dying by how they stick to me like glue," she laughed. "They don't even want to leave the house! That's why I am so glad Amber is here with them. She makes them go outside and play with her." She chuckled, "That Amber is more like you, than you are like you right now."

"I know," I laughed. "She takes everything in stride and keeps on trucking. I used to have that kind of faith that everything was going to be okay. I guess I need to get back to that."

"Yeah, that childlike faith… I know you think I don't pray because I don't go to church a lot," she raised her hand to stop my protest - I closed my mouth and let her continue, "but I pray all the time. I read my word and pray with the children, it's just that working on Sundays at the hospital just wouldn't allow me to go to church consistently and even though we didn't need the money, I

167

couldn't leave my patients to another doctor. Since I've been home sick, I haven't had the strength to leave the house to be honest. I'm glad Bishop came to see me in the hospital and had made sure I get communion. He understands."

"Come on Mishie, I'm not judging you. I know what you do and why. I just know that for me, going to church consistently helps sustain my faith when I am going through a crisis."

"Well, I understand that for sure. I just I know my faith is strong, now more than any time in my life. I haven't broken down like I thought I would at this point. At first, I thought it was shock, but I realized today that it's my faith in action."

"You've always been the strong one Mishie. Always." I shook my head to stop the tears and leaned my head back so that my mascara wouldn't run.

"What's that on your neck Neene?"

"What?"

"It looks like hand prints Neene! What happened?"

"Jon and I got into it on the way home from County. I think he got it out of his system now though, it was the first and last time he put his hands on me, and I have to admit, I thought he was going to kill me on the side of the road Mishie."

"Wait!" Mishie sat up on her chaise, her neck wrenched to the side as she looked at me. "You finally told him the truth? All of it?"

"Yes."

Mishie closed her eyes momentarily then slowly opened them. "I don't know what to say Neene. I didn't think he would do something like this, I knew he would be mad, but... Are you all right?"

"I guess... I feel set adrift in a way. I kinda feel strangely at peace at the same time. It's like I haven't given up, but I'm resigned to allow God to do His will as

I'm concerned and not struggle with my own foolishness anymore."

"I know what you mean, I'd been struggling for so long with telling the kids and consumed with how they would take it and what they would do without me, but the other day, I just knelt down and prayed after everyone had gone to work and school. I asked God to allow me to be free from the worry about what would happen when I was gone, so that I could enjoy my last days here with my children."

"Did he answer?"

"Not exactly, but I felt more at ease that day and I felt my joy coming back. I guess it's true that your joy is your strength. I told the kids that one day soon, mommy would go to heaven to be with God, but daddy would be here with them."

I thought about what would happen if my marriage split up and if Jon would carry through with his threat of taking the children from me in divorce. How would my children take it? How would I survive without them? Would I still be allowed to run the Center at the church? There was so much at stake! "What did the children say when you said that?"

"They cried, then they just held onto me tightly for about an hour. When one stopped crying the other would start. If it wasn't so sad and morbid, it would have been *funny* - Girl, they were in a relay race to see how wet my shirt could get! I was crying myself though chile; the love I felt pouring from them was overwhelming." Her eyes filled up with tears and she looked away.

"Hey… You guys want anything to drink?" Marcus said from the doorway, startling us.

I jerkily spun around in my seat to see his face and replied, "I'm good Marcus, thanks."

Mishie said, "I'd like some lemonade baby, thank you." Then as he walked off, she said, "I didn't even know he was home!"

I was too busy wondering how long he had been standing there and how much he'd heard.

***

That Wednesday, I made my way to Dr. Williams' office for the last time feeling mixed about what was about to happen. It had been a little over a week since the altercation with Robert and Jon; things at home have been akin to walking around trying not to piss the ground off; fuses were short all around and in two weeks Jon Jr. was coming home. We needed closure.

I parked my car in the same spot I did on the initial visit and found myself wondering what had really changed for me internally from these sessions. Had she helped me in any way deal with my inability to be faithful? I'm at a loss on what to do about where my life is right now, so I think my husband is right; we need spiritual guidance from the one who joined us and has known us for the past nineteen years. I gathered my scattered musings in the silence of my Lexus; it was time to end this leg of the journey.

Dr. Williams' office was the same, but I realized that I still didn't know if the man in the picture on her desk was her brother or lover and I still didn't know if all of this was worth it.

"Hello Janine. How are you feeling today?"

"I don't know doctor. I feel like it may have been a waste of time to be honest. My life has come apart more than it has come together since I've been in therapy with you."

"I can see why you would see things that way, Janine. The thing about therapy is that you have to put into action the things we talk about in therapy, in your walk in the world. Can you say that you have?"

"Can I say I've what?"

"Can you say that you have put the effort into being monogamous and making your marriage work or at least coming to grips with the whys of your actions and a way to change them in the future?"

170

Had I? I can say for sure that the monogamy is in my heart and my actions will reflect that from now on, because although it hasn't been that long, I have no desire for any other man aside from my husband. I guess that what they call baby-steps. I most definitely can say I have taken steps to make my marriage work and am willing to do whatever it will take for it to be a success, but the last part... I just don't know if I have a way to change my actions in the future. Even though I now know that my father's absence broke me in some ways, I don't know if these sessions gave me the tools to fix myself in a way that I won't make the same missteps again, but I do know that the clarity I've gained here and from my study of the Word through Bishop's sermons have been working on my perspective of myself and my role as a wife, mother and partner.

"I don't think so. I now know the whys, but I'm still working on how to avoid falling and failing my family again."

"What about the monogamy matter?"

"Well, we talked about the sex with others the last time and I haven't been with any other man side from my husband since, nor do I desire to, so I'm doing better at curbing the promiscuity and lack of boundaries that plagued me before."

"Well, that is progress Janine! We've had three sessions over four weeks and although it may seem like a long time, it's really not in comparison to the time you had to learn and enact those behaviors that got you into this predicament in the first place."

"I didn't think about it like that doctor."

"So, I gave you a thought stopping tool - Do you remember it?"

"No. I really don't recall Dr. Williams; refresh my memory. So much has happened in the last few days..." I said adjusting the Chanel, black and white insignia scarf I had around my neck.

"I asked you to think about your family before you make any and every decision. To think about them before you brush your teeth, before you comb your hair; to put them first in everything that you do. I wanted you to see that when you put your own desires to the side, it can help you stop the behaviors that got you here."

"Actually doctor, I have been doing that! Although I can't say it's been with every decision, I have been incorporating it more and more every day because I realized that what will make them happy, makes me happy. I want my children and husband to know that I love them with my actions. It's funny because even the sermons at church seem to be giving me affirmation and confirmation about my new decision making paradigm."

"Great! Give me a scenario where you recently put them first in something that seemed mundane or even against what you wanted, but you could see it made a difference to them."

"Well doctor, I have been thinking about what I make for dinner trying to be more accommodating to what they need and want as well as what their favorites are when I create my weekly menu and do my grocery shopping. I know it seems silly…"

"No." Dr. Williams cut me off abruptly. "That is exactly what I needed to see in reference to your changing your outlook and perspective from one that is 'me' centered to one that is 'us' or even 'family' centered. Good work! The next question is; how do you know it made a difference to them?"

"Jon noticed that I'd bought his favorite fruit: strawberries, which I hate. I don't usually even bother buying them because they go bad so easily and he's not usually at home to eat them. Amber was so happy I made her favorite desert – pineapple upside down cake, the other day… It really felt good to make them feel good and know that I think about them."

"Great. What does it feel like when they express their gratitude?"

"It made me feel proud of myself, of my ability to make them happy with the small things."

"What about your decision to stay with your husband? Is that to make them happy or is it to make you happy?"

I didn't know what to say. At first thought it was to make myself happy, but when I really thought about it, it was more about us as a whole, which includes me. "Well, I have to say that I get the point. My family includes me, so what I do for myself has to include them, because I am an integral part of it, not an entity unto myself. I may have my separate needs but even in those, I have to consider their needs and expectations of me if not first, simultaneously."

"Yes. That is a great way for us to end our sessions. I am just hopeful that the road you are on is one that you continue to travel Janine. It's important that we live honestly with ourselves and with others. This treatment, at its core, was to allow you to look at your past and its influences on your life, see your behavior with a somewhat objective view and how your actions have and will affect those you care about."

"Thank you Dr. Williams." As I rose to leave, I thought about the fact that I really was helped by these sessions, even though just an hour ago I couldn't pinpoint their effect on my life. I fought against the therapy because of my shame and my unwillingness to consider that what I was doing was unjustifiable. Even in my husband's betrayal and absence, I was not released from my duties as a wife and mother.

***

"So, how was your last session?" Jon asked as soon as I walked in the door that evening.

"It was enlightening. I can't wait to hear what Bishop has to say," I said sitting my purse down on the kitchen counter.

"I'm glad it was helpful. To be honest, I just did it to shame you, I felt like you really played me and I wanted to make you feel worse by having to go and talk to someone about being a sex addict."

"Well, whatever your reasoning, it made me realize that what I was doing was putting myself before everyone else, even God. I think now is the best time for us to go and meet with Bishop. I truly think you would have benefited from the sessions with Dr. Williams too. You could have explored why you thought it was okay to have two families and not be honest to me about having a son," I said as I washed my hands in the kitchen sink and poured myself a glass of iced tea.

"What? How dare you come at me like that after all...?"

"Really Jon? Whatever. You're being really self-righteous right now. Yeah, I stepped out on our marriage but you were already stepping out; you had *been* stepped out."

"You know what Neene? Please. I don't have to have this conversation with you," he turned to leave the kitchen shaking his head.

"You may think you don't. You may think that you're the lesser of two evils, but I want you to know that *you* being an adulterer, and *me* being an adulterer is the same adulterous behavior. Just because you are a Deacon in *The Lord's Church* doesn't make you exempt from the sin."

"You brazen hussy," he said, turning back to face me, teeth clenched. "You think I believe I'm exempt because I'm a deacon? I'm not exempt of the lies I've told to try to keep my family together, but I did not sleep with Leslie over the past nineteen years. I am not going to say it was easy to maintain that boundary with her; after all, I left her for you because you were my dream woman. I didn't even know she was pregnant until after I found out you were and had already proposed." He went to fridge, grabbed a beer, slammed the refrigerator door and sat his beer down on the counter with a loud thud – suds spilling over his fisted knuckles went unnoticed.

"Would you have chosen her if you'd known she was pregnant before you left her for me?" I asked watching the suds slide onto the counter.

"Probably. Especially if I had known that you and Robert had been together."

Wow! 'I could really lose my husband to this other family," I thought then said, "Things probably would have been totally different if we had all been honest with one another from the start."

"Maybe so, but we were all young and wanted what we wanted. Now we all have to deal with the present as it is. All I know is that I want to keep my family and I want to make sure that we make it Neene. Look at Marc and Misch man. We had that, didn't we? What happened to us?"

"I don't know Jon. I want what you want, but I want you to *really forgive* me."

"I forgave you Neene. That's not the problem I'm having. I'm having a serious problem dealing with your constant betrayal over the past nineteen years. I'm not sure what to do about how I feel every time I look at my son. I talked to Bishop about it and he said that it's part of the healing process and learning to trust you again, but he also said that you are going through the same thing with me, so I have to be mindful of my own betrayal of you."

"I'm glad he said that. When did he say we could meet with him? I think we need to do it really soon... I'm going to get Amber," I drank the last of my tea and sat my glass in the sink.

"How did you do it Neene?" Jon said taking a sip of his beer watching me walk away, eyes slits.

"What?" I replied as I gathered my things and heading out of the door.

"How did you look me in the face every day and not think about what you were doing to me?"

"How did I look in your face every day knowing that you were in North Carolina with your other woman, when you said you were working? Is that what you asked me?" I said dropping my purse on the kitchen counter stool and turning to face him with my hands on my hips.

"I didn't say that to make you angry Neene; I said it to because that is what I ask myself every day."

"Well, if you really want to know how I did it, ask yourself." I said as I grabbed my purse and walked out of the door.

I walked down the block a bit and stopped. The tears I'd dammed up streamed down my face. I was steaming! How dare he act like what he did was okay and what I did was unforgivable? On one hand I felt like he was worse than I, he hid a whole family and another life. Whether he slept with Leslie or not, was irrelevant; it was the sharing of time and space that hurt more than if he had slept with her. Plus, because of the child they shared, there was no way that their interactions would stop. I would have to live with the fact that he had another family forever. Robert and I were done and although we are dealing with getting him out of our lives for good, eventually, he will go away forever, but this boy, this *other* son; he'll be with us until we go to the grave.

I barely made it through rest of the workweek at the shelter. My spirit was so heavy with frustration about the situation I'd put my family in, I couldn't wait to get to church to give it all to God. I made it through the doors of the sanctuary and sighed with relief. The presence of The Lord was already there. The praise and worship team had everyone already on their feet giving God the glory He deserved! I got to the second pew with all of the other Deacon's wives and children, sat my purse down and stood singing and praising The Lord with fresh tears in my eyes. When Bishop Brown finally came out, I was still on my feet. At this point, the entire church was crying out "Halleluiah!" and praising His Holy Name in worship of our Savior; we were fired up!

Bishop Brown stepped up to the pulpit, "The Holy Ghost is ministering right now, but I also have a word from The Lord. Turn your bibles to 1st Samuel Chapter 1 verses 1-20. I will read aloud while you read silently. *The Birth of Samuel, 1 There was a certain man from Ramathaim, a Zuphite[a] from the hill country of Ephraim, whose name was Elkanah son of Jeroham, the son of Elihu, the son of Tohu, the son of Zuph, an Ephraimite. 2 He had two wives; one was called Hannah and the other Peninnah. Peninnah had children, but Hannah had none. 3 Year after year this man went up from his town to worship and sacrifice to the Lord Almighty at Shiloh, where Hophni and Phinehas, the two sons of Eli, were priests of the Lord. 4 Whenever the day came for Elkanah to sacrifice, he would give portions of the meat to his wife Peninnah and to all her sons and daughters. 5 But to Hannah he gave a double portion because he loved her, and the Lord had closed her womb. 6 Because the Lord had closed Hannah's womb, her rival kept provoking her in order to irritate her. 7 This went on year after year. Whenever Hannah went up to the house of the Lord, her rival provoked her till she wept and would not eat. 8 Her husband Elkanah would say to her, "Hannah, why are you weeping? Why don't you eat? Why are you downhearted? Don't I mean more to you than ten sons?" 9 Once when they had finished eating and drinking in Shiloh, Hannah stood up. Now Eli the priest was sitting on his chair by the doorpost of the Lord's house. 10 In her deep anguish Hannah prayed to the Lord, weeping bitterly. 11 And she made a vow, saying, "Lord Almighty, if you will only look on your servant's misery and remember me, and not forget your servant but give her a son, then I will give him to the Lord for all the days of his life, and no razor will ever be used on his head." 12 As she kept on praying to the Lord, Eli observed her mouth. 13 Hannah was praying in her heart, and her lips were moving but her voice was not heard. Eli thought she was drunk 14 and said to her, "How long are you going to stay drunk? Put away your wine." 15 "Not so, my lord," Hannah replied, "I am a woman who is deeply troubled. I have not been drinking wine or beer; I was pouring out my soul to the Lord. 16 Do not take your servant for a wicked woman; I have been praying here out of my great anguish and grief." 17 Eli answered, "Go in peace, and may the God of Israel grant you what you have asked of him." 18 She said, "May your servant find favor in your eyes." Then she went her way and ate something, and her face was no longer downcast. 19 Early the next morning they arose and worshiped before the Lord and then went back to their home at Ramah. Elkanah made love to his wife Hannah, and the Lord remembered her. 20 So in the course of time Hannah became pregnant and gave birth to a son. She named him Samuel, saying, "Because I asked the Lord for him."*

Everyone prayed together and then the congregation settled down for the lesson we were about to be taught. Bishop Brown began to relay the story back to us and for a moment, I drifted. When I looked in front of me and saw my husband, then to my left and saw my babygirl, we looked like the perfect family, even without JD being there. The church's stained glass windows of Jesus' life glinted in the sun and the Resurrection scene to the right of the pulpit caught my attention. I usually focused on the sacrifice, the crucifixion scene, as it reminded me of His outpouring of love for me but today, another resurrection was on my mind; my own.

"She is frustrated and because she is, the entire family is frustrated. Not only in their day to day lives, but in their worship," said Bishop Brown, and my ears immediately returned to the lesson at hand. "The problem with frustration is that it's quietly submerged into the subconscious mind and it's based on unresolved anger. This is where the enemy gets his hold on you. The anger. The anger you are no longer focused on because it's become embedded and now presents as frustration. Now, I am not saying you aren't supposed to feel anger! You are, but feel it and sin not because once you hold on to it – it becomes a stronghold and that – that is what frustration really is! *A stronghold*!"

Wow. "There are many, many reasons we fall victim to this kind of anger: when people don't see situations like we do, when we get impatient, when we have a timetable of when things should happen and they don't, when we have a general sense of unfairness about how life is and how things have happened to us," said Bishop Brown, now getting into the meat of the lesson.

Amber said, " Mommy. I have to go pee-pee. Mommy... Take me to potty now please!"

"Wait a minute baby, Mommy needs to hear this, just give me a minute." Jon cut his eyes at both of us silencing her, but making me give him the fish-eyed stare. How dare he?

Sister Jolene, sitting directly in behind me leaned in and whispered to me, "I'll take her, Janine. Sierra has to go too," little Amber scooted out of the pew to Sister Jolene and was led out with her and daughter.

Bishop was saying, "...He had two wives. Hannah, his favorite, was unable to bear children and that was why he married Peninnah in the first place. To do what Hannah couldn't. Even though she could never replace Hannah in his heart, she had a way to frustrate Hannah – because of her children. Even though Hannah was the center of attention, even though Hannah got a double portion as if she had children and even though it was obvious who Elkanah loved the most, Hannah was still frustrated. She had the best of him and from him, but she still wasn't satisfied. Because she couldn't bear children."

Why was I frustrated? I had to sit and ask myself that. I was. I had been... It wasn't so much the other son, although he has been added to my recent frustrations. It was because I was left alone for so long and I thought it was unfair. I thought that even though he gave me his best, what I really wanted I couldn't have and I made my decision to stray out of the frustration I felt instead of coming to him or better yet, going to God!

Bishop Brown said, "...God was the only one Hannah could have gone to, to fix her closed womb! Every no from God, is not a never, sometimes it's a *not right now*! Sometimes God wants you to get your character in order. So, while He's saying no, He's waiting and watching to see what you are going to do. Will you sin?

Will make poor decisions? Will you sacrifice your family's peace for you to satisfy your frustrations? You can't move to a new level with old behaviors!"

By this time the half the church was on its feet and the traditional call and response had begun, "Amen Bishop! Yes Lord! Fix me Lord! You're teaching sir!" Were the punctuation marks for his every pause for breath.

"Hannah figured out she had to cry out to The Lord! She realized she was risking everything in her frustration and was *about to lose it all*! She went to The Lord and made Him a promise – If you ever want to The Lord to bless you – *obligate Him*! She promised to give her son back to Him, which involved God in the outcome of her blessing! She made a vow that He would get glory from and she was joined by the man of God in her prayer! If you ever want to be blessed, *give Him all you have!* *Hannah rose up* from the depths of her crying and frustration. *Hannah rose up* again and went back to her family to join them in worship, *Hannah rose up again* and went home and lay with her husband, *Hannah rose up again* and she kept on rising! She rose above her frustration and God remembered her! He not only remembered her once – He remembered five more times! Hannah means grace and five is not only the number of grace, it's the number of children Hannah bore after being barren!"

By this time the organ chords are jumping and the church seems to be swaying on its very foundation. Bishop is chanting, *"Keep rising Hannah. Keep rising. Keep rising Hannah. Keep rising,"* and I am out of my seat with tears on my face and a dance in my feet.

CHAPTER 22

Jon: Making A Man

We made our way to the Bishop's office on Sunday after serving in service and we were still barely speaking. Amber was quiet and watchful when in the same room with us and JD was due home in two-week's time. We needed an intervention now. I was kind of glad they gave him an extra week of therapy to work on perfecting his walking with the prosthetic. Even though I know it was partly my fault, I couldn't bring myself to get past the fact that my son isn't really mine. Then, it's like Neene's attitude about what she's done to our family is like, '*So what. It's done; let's move on.*' And I am just not sure I can.

I sat down at the table in the conference room off of Bishop's office and Neene sat opposite me. She refused to look me in the eyes, but I couldn't keep my eyes off of her. She looked just as good as she did when we met, just seasoned and even more beautiful. I was confused and conflicted because I hated her and simultaneously, I still loved her the same.

181

"Good afternoon," Bishop said as he walked into the room having changed out of his pulpit attire and into a three-piece, navy blue, silk suit replete with a matching vest and gold bow tie. "How are you all doing today? How's JD coming along?" He asked as he sat at the head of the table.

Neene finally looked up and replied, "JD's coming home in about two weeks Bishop and we need to get some things between us settled before he does."

"Well, Sister Janine, I can't promise you a miracle of complete healing in a two-week time frame, but I can assure you that we will be well on the road of bringing some closure and resolution to whatever is going on between you two before JD gets back."

"I hope so," I replied. *That's exactly what I need: closure and resolution.'* I thought to myself.

"So do I," replied Janine, cutting her eyes at me. "I don't want to walk into the house and feel this wave of mistrust and anger when I look in his face anymore Bishop."

"Well, I don't want to feel that way about you either honestly, but I can't hide it. And to be honest, how the hell am I supposed to feel after what you've done?"

"Ask yourself that question Jon! How am I supposed to feel?"

"So," Bishop broke in, stretching the "o" sound out. "What I hear you both saying is that you feel betrayed by the other. Is this correct?"

"Yes," we responded together.

"Okay good. You are on one accord with something. Now, we are going to work on getting you back on one accord completely." He nodded his head briefly, went to his desk and picked up a black leather journal. "First things first," he said as he took out a black and gold pen and began to write. "Nothing that we say here can be repeated to anyone other than who is in the room right now. Confidentiality has to be strictly maintained, so that the process of healing can be uninterrupted by those who have no stake in the outcome. Agreed?"

"Aight. I'll keep everything to myself." I replied long after Neene had said okay and they were both looking at me expectantly. I was slow on the yes with this one, because I told Marc everything. I could see where this could be a problem though, because he tells Mishie everything. *'What in the world was Bishop writing in that book of his?'*

"Is there a problem with doing that Jon?" asked Bishop, with his eyebrow raised.

"No, no... I just had to process it fully. I don't have a problem with keeping what happens here confidential at all."

"Okay, that is the only rule aside from if I feel that either of you pose a physical threat to one another or yourselves, I would have to report that to the authorities; after speaking with you about my concerns of course."

"Okay," Neene and I said together, but in the back of my mind, I wondered if my forcing myself on her would come up or if she would tell Bishop about my wrapping my hands around her throat. Hearing the words authorities made me flinch. The authorities have no idea what I really want to do to her behind, or I would already be in jail.

"These are the ground rules. Are you guys okay with moving forward?"

"Yes," we both replied.

"Now, this is spiritual based counseling, which means when there is any disagreement about how to proceed in how you relate to one another, I am going to go to the manual for our lives and see what God says. And we all know what the manual is right?"

"Yes Bishop, of course." Neene answered sounding irritated and rolling her eyes at me like I was the one who said it. I just nodded and ignored her, turning my head and attention to Bishop.

"Okay, now, I just want to make sure because we aren't going to be reading from the First Book of Janine, verse nine or the Book of Dupont, Chapter seven or even the Book of Bishop; it will be the word of God."

I could see that this was going to be a little more difficult than I first envisioned. He made it sound simple, but usually when he did that it meant it was going to be a rough ride. I remember when I first came to this church, it was before Janine and I got married. We had come together; or rather she brought me to church with her because I wasn't too keen on God after seeing my God-fearing father work himself into an early grave. She had been attending the church since her freshman year at Spelman and knew many of the people at the church by that point.

When she introduced me to Bishop, as everyone affectionately called him, his first question was: "Do you love the Lord Jon?"

All I could say was, "Yes. Bishop Sir, I do love The Lord." Though at the time I wasn't so sure how I felt about God, Bishop changed all of that. I know my father must be happy in heaven to see me being an upstanding Deacon in The Lord's Church these past 10 years.

He replied, "I just want to make sure you do, because Janine here, she's one of His children and she loves Him dearly. Plus, she's one of my adopted Spelman daughters and I love her dearly too. So that means you are going to have to show me you love The Lord like you say you do, in order to stay an integral part of Janine's life."

He was right and sitting in this office right now, I remember that when we stayed connected to God, we stayed connected to one another a whole lot better.

"So, I'm going to start with asking you both a question – What do you want to achieve from these sessions with me? What is your goal?" Bishop broke into my thoughts. "I want you to answer this individually, in that I want you to answer only thinking about what you need, not what the marriage needs." He paused and looked at our faces and seemingly sensed our reluctance to share in front of one another. "If you want, I can have one leave the room so that the other doesn't feel intimidated with their answer."

"I don't need to have her leave. She already knows what I want. I want these sessions to help me not only understand why she did what she did, but I want help with forgiving her for what she's done to my trust and my love."

"Okay," he said nodding and taking brief notes as he looked at Neene expectantly.

"I just want to move past all of this and get back to the good times we used to share before all of this drama. I want to feel good about us."

"Hmmm… Okay. The goals of marriage counseling, even from a Christian perspective, is to help facilitate communication that is going to be beneficial to the building or rebuilding of your marriage and not contribute to the tearing down of one another, thus destroying what you both are here to preserve. Now, I am going to give you both an opportunity to tell me what circumstances brought you here, but there are ground rules to this sharing. The first rule is that if one person has the floor, the other person must stay silent until they are done, no matter how upset what they are hearing makes them feel. The second is that we must be respectful in our retelling: meaning we won't use expletives or any disparaging talk about our partner. That's it. Jon you go first."

"I have to sit here and listen to him tear me down? That's not fair Bishop!" She rolled her eyes and sucked her teeth.

"Well… Maybe he won't. Plus, remember he will have to listen to your side of what has transpired as well, so be open to listening, not defending. You will have ten minutes apiece to tell me what has brought you here. Jon, are you ready to share?" He said as he got up, went to his desk to get the timer, set it, then placed it on conference table.

She makes me sick sometimes, sounding like a spoiled brat. The nerve. She has me raising somebody else's child as my own and she doesn't want to be torn down? Whatever. I'm going first. "Yes. I'm ready to share." I said glaring at Janine. Then I continued, "Bishop, I found out that my son wasn't mine in the hospital right after he had his leg amputated! I wasn't able to donate blood to him and neither was Janine because he has O-positive blood and neither of us do."

"Okay. How did that make you feel? What was your reaction?"

"I felt betrayed, used, like a damn fool to be honest. I wondered how she could be my wife; live with our children and me, when she knew that he wasn't mine all along. I didn't want to be in her presence, but we had to save face for JD because there was no way I was going to allow her being a whore make my son falter in his recovery."

"Jon. Now, I've already warned you. None of that will be allowed." Bishop said shaking his head and looking at Janine's face crumple and her eyes fill with tears.

"Okay, I apologize – but the funny thing was that I was with the birth father when I got to the hospital and didn't know it. I was asking him to investigate her for sleeping with someone else! My son's birth father was my best friend or rather ex-best friend from college. I had no idea that she was with him right before she was my girl back then, or I probably wouldn't have even dated her, much less married her." I looked over at Janine and her eyes were wide; she looked astonished, like she couldn't believe I would tell Bishop everything, but I wasn't finished.

"What was your reaction?"

"That night we found out, I immediately wanted to embarrass her and I also wanted to have some grounds for divorce, so I called my lawyer and had him put a contract together that stipulated that if she didn't attend sex-addiction counseling that she would forfeit her rights to the children and to any alimony from me in divorce. I honestly thought she would never sign the agreement or go to the sessions. I thought she would just leave the kids and me, continue with her shelter and go on with her life with her other man, but I was wrong."

"What was your plan if she did that? If she left you and the kids, what were you going to do?"

"I was going to go and marry Leslie and move the kids to South Carolina so that my whole family could be one." I heard Janine sob as I said that last line and I felt badly for her for about a split second. Then, I felt vindicated. It was the truth. "I was going to introduce my children to their brother and start over, but she surprised me and went through with the therapy."

"What did you think when she went through with it?" Bishop asked watching Janine intently.

"I was confused. I didn't know what to think. I wanted to believe that she loved me, but I thought that perhaps she just wanted to stay for the kids or because of the money I had and the lifestyle I afford her." I shook my head, not being unsure of what her motives were made me feel crazy.

"So what happened next? How did we get here?"

"Well, things were really tense at home; I couldn't stand the sight of her but still wanted her physically at the same time. I was still having her investigated, so when Robert called me in for the discovery meeting, then insinuated that he was my son's real dad and told me that he had her on tape having sex with him; I tried to kill him and he had me arrested. I know you saw it on the news Bishop – I saw you'd called me when I got home, but Neene was the only one I could reach who could pick me up from the police station. I wanted to kill her so bad – I really just wanted to kill both of 'em." My fist pounded the mahogany meeting table so hard the water glasses shook. "I sat in that cell waiting for her behind for two whole hours and all I saw was their blood on my hands."

"Well, Jon are you past those feelings?" Bishop asked earnestly. I could tell he was contemplating having *"that talk"* with me about the authorities and such.

"I think so Bishop. I just feel really hurt and confused mostly now. The feeling of betrayal by a loved one is like a wound that never heals because the person is still there ripping the scab off over and over."

"Where are you now emotionally, besides feeling betrayed and hurt?"

"I'm at the place where I want closure or at least an explanation that I can understand."

"Well, your ten minutes are up now. It's time to let Janine tell her side of the story. Are you ready?" He asked turning to her.

She wiped her eyes and stared at me angrily. "Now that he's finished ripping me to shreds, can I respond to some of the things he said Bishop?" Janine said glaring, her red-rimmed eyes pointed and tore at me.

"No Neene," Bishop said clearly surprised by her childish behavior. "You can only tell your own version of why you think you are here."

"Okay fine. Well... I know we are here because of me. I understand I made some choices that were against the covenant I made with my husband and I admit that. I just want to be clear that I married him while I was still in love with someone else. I shouldn't have, but I wanted a certain life for myself and a certain kind of man and Jon was it. After I'd gotten my heart broken, I was numb. I didn't come to him or our relationship knowing I was pregnant by Robert, I found out I was pregnant afterwards and there wasn't a way to know whose baby it was to be honest; there was a month window where it was fair game. So just like he came to our relationship with some strings, so did I. Robert called me and apologized and cried on the phone and I refused to see him. I wanted him to hurt like I did when I found out about his girlfriend, but when he got arrested I felt so bad, that I went to the court dates. I sat in the back to silently offer him my prayers and support hoping he wouldn't notice, but he did."

"Why did you hope he wouldn't notice?"

"I guess I didn't want him to think I wanted to start back up with him, I was happy and in love with Jon at the time – I just felt bad that Robert was having such a hard life in the meantime. But then I started to get letters from him and I was vulnerable; I was home alone with JD so much and Jon was always working and in South Carolina... Or rather, acting like he was working but really with his other family in South Carolina." She said looking at me with her lips twisted up in a smirk then continued, "The attention Robert gave me, and the things he said in his letters were a temptation I succumbed to. Then he came home, and I guess where I'd opened the door just a crack with the letters, he just bust it wide open when I met with him the first time."

"When did you meet with him for the first time? How long ago was it?"

"It was only a little over five years ago. He just showed up outside my job one day with flowers wanting to take me to lunch. I was shocked, I mean I hadn't given him my job's address, but then I didn't know he had been home for a while and had started a private investigation firm either. He just walked back into my life filling a void that Jon left with his long absences..."

"C'mon Neene! Really? You can't be serious. I called you all of the time when I was away! In front of Leslie! She knew she didn't have a chance, but you made him think he did – that's why he thought he could just show up!" I couldn't take it anymore. Making me feel like I abandoned her, when she knows damn well I didn't!

"Jon, you have to let her finish. She allowed you to talk uninterrupted, please give her the same respect."

"I apologize Bishop," I replied shaking my head and went back to trying to tune her out.

"Okay Neene, is there anything else you'd like to add?"

"I just wanted to say that I'm not putting what I did on Robert or Jon. I did it and I'm sorry that I did this to us, it was immature to just lash out and try to get back at him that way, but when Robert showed me those pictures of you and Leslie..." She'd turned to talk to me directly. "I just wanted to get back at you. Now, I just want to go back to loving you and for things to go back to the way they were when JD was smaller and we were happy." She started crying and Bishop stood, his barely tan face turning slightly red, handed her some tissues and began rubbing and patting her back.

He rubbed his beard and then said, "Now, I'm need to talk to you both separately for a few minutes. Who wants to go first? Matter of fact, let's toss a coin." He proceeded to take a half dollar out of his vest pocket and flip in the air, "Heads Jon; tails Janine." He deftly caught it and laid it on the back of his other hand. It was heads. I couldn't help but think that this was something he had done countless times in his counseling of the various couples in our church and in his practice.

"So, I guess that means it's on me." I said staring unseeingly at the various plaques and awards that graced the walls on his office. I wasn't sure I wanted to share what was weighing on me but I had no other way to deal with it.

"When's my turn Bishop?" Janine asked as she stood, wiped her eyes and went to the door avoiding eye contact with me.

"Oh you are going to wait outside for about thirty minutes while I talk to Jon, then he is going to wait for you. Patience practiced is how it becomes a fruit of the spirit. The kids are all picked up and everything right? I have this time to clear and free spend with you guys?" He said with his eyebrows raised, he loved our children and was so saddened by JD's public loss. He went to as

190

many games as he could when JD played in the varsity championship.

"Yes, the kids have a sitter and we cleared an hour and a half for this first session as you told us…" Neene replied.

"Right, so go on outside and don't go too far now Neene, the thirty minutes are going to go a lot faster than you think."

Janine walked out of the office saying, "I'm going to the church café to read until it's my turn. Text me when you're coming out Jon, and I'll be right in."

"Okay," I replied.

"Alright Jon, you did okay for a while there. I know it was difficult listening to her say those things, but is there anything you want to share that you felt you couldn't in front of Janine?"

"Yes… I don't know what to do about my son."

"In what respect? Wait. Are you speaking of JD or Jacob?"

"I'm talking about Jacob. I don't know what to do about maintaining contact with him after him being part of the cause of JD's accident. I've been talking to him on the phone, but I'm not sure if I want to go back down there for a while."

"Jon, they are both yours, one by choice and circumstance and the other by birth. Do you think either deserves to be left to grow up without your guidance?"

"No… But I am unsure of what to do about integrating him into my family. I really thought about divorcing Neene, taking the kids down there and marrying Leslie. She would be with it. I haven't been really paying her any mind, but Marcus made it plain to me that she's been waiting for me. All of these years, just waiting for the off chance that I would want her…"

"Do you?"

"Do I what?"

"Do you want Leslie? I ask because she was a big part of your after divorce scenario."

"No, but I do want my son to be taken good care of though. I pay for their expenses because I want my son to be afforded a lifestyle similar to my other children. I mean… I don't want her, I want Neene, but she could be a runner-up. She's always been a runner-up, because I've always had the first place prize in my possession, so she didn't really matter."

"Do you feel as if you no longer have the first place prized possession?"

"In a way… I feel like I was made a fool of, like I was played and they were laughing at me behind my back when they were together. I feel like she was his and never really mine at all."

"When Neene was telling her side of the story did you hear her say that she loved you and wanted to be with you?"

I had to pause. Did she say that? "I don't recall her saying that Bishop. I honestly don't."

"She did… On two separate occasions." He said glancing through his black leather-bound notebook, the pages turning quickly as he read through them, then peered at me over his horn-rimmed glasses. "What do you think about that?"

"That maybe she really does love me…"

"She really said it… Do you feel safe enough to trust her? She wasn't asked directly about whether she loved you or not, she said it in the course of her explaining what happened."

"I don't feel safe enough to trust her. I want to though. I want to believe that my wife loves me and wants me."

"Well, she's said both of those things. When do you think you will be able to get back to trusting her? Have you truly forgiven her? Maybe that's too many questions at once." He paused briefly, "Take a stab at either of them or both if you think you can."

"I don't know about the when question, but I want to forgive her right now for good."

"Why?"

"Why what Bishop?"

"Why do you want to forgive her? Why right now?"

"Because I don't want to have this conflict in my mind when it comes to her. It's making me feel crazy."

"Well that is one definition of insanity: to be conflicted without resolution. Being torn between two choices can literally drive you crazy. The trick is that you have to remember you have the power to make a decision to not only forgive her, but to trust her at any time."

"What do you mean Bishop? I have the power... The power as in what?" I was confused as all get out. I mean c'mon man, this is not Greyskull and I am not He-Man. I feel completely powerless.

"As in, you have the decision making power to forgive her and to trust her. She didn't have to go through with the therapy. She didn't have to say that she loves you and wants things to go back to when you two were happy. Those things she said without prompting. She also took responsibility for what has happened. What does she have to do for you to make those decisions?"

"I don't know Bishop... I'm not sure."

"If you don't know, then how are you supposed to know when you have the closure you say you want?"

That was a good question. How was I supposed to know? I couldn't answer. The silence spread around the office, thick like fresh ground peanut butter and crunchy; filled with the thoughts I had scattered in my mind.

Bishop broke into the silence with another question, "So, Jon, why did you get married?"

"What do you mean Bishop? I love Janine. I wanted to make our family official." At least that was an easy question.

"Those are good reasons. Why did you love Janine then?"

"Because she was beautiful, smart; she had ambition and drive. She was easy to be myself around and she encouraged me in whatever I was doing, whether it was school or starting my business."

"Has any of that changed? The reasons that you loved her, have they changed?"

I was stuck. I really couldn't say they had if that was the criteria for my loving her, so I replied, "No, but…"

"No buts, if they have changed that's fine, but there are no buts. Maybe there's more to it than that?"

"Yeah, there is more… I loved her because she seemed like the perfect wife. She cooked, she didn't start crazy arguments, she loved our son and took care of our home. She respected me and made me feel like a man."

"Okay. Now we are getting somewhere. She fit into the mold of what you thought a perfect wife would be then? What about now? What does a perfect marriage look like? I gave you guys some scriptures during your pre-marital counseling: Peter 3:7-9. Let's turn to that one now. You did bring your bible, right Jon?"

"Yes, I have a bible app on my phone Bishop," I replied as I opened my Bible app and quickly pulled up the scripture. I did remember reading this scripture, but it's one so infrequently taught in service or in Bible study that it hadn't been reinforced or impressed upon my mind like it should have.

Bishop began reading from The Word:"7 Husbands, in the same way be considerate as you live with your wives, and treat them with respect as the weaker partner and as heirs with you of the gracious gift of life, so that nothing will hinder your prayers. 8 Finally, all of you, be like-minded, be sympathetic, love one another, be compassionate and humble. 9 Do not repay evil with evil or insult with insult. On the contrary, repay evil with blessing, because to this you were called so that you may inherit a blessing…" He paused and asked, "What do you think? How do you think this applies to your marriage?"

194

I read and then re-read that passage and conviction fell on me like a heavy rain. All of the times I wasn't compassionate to her pleas for me to come home, how I just disregarded her feelings in favor of the money I was making or the time I wanted to spend with my son in South Carolina. At the same time, I also felt like she repaid my evil for evil instead of a blessing. I was wrong, but she made things ten times worse by doing what she did. "I think we both may have dropped the ball on this one Bishop," I replied.

"Yes, I think you both just may have. Now is the time to pick up the ball and get back into the game. Are you ready?"

"Yes, I think I am."

"Great! Our time is just about up for now, so do me a favor and text Janine for me."

"Doing it right now Bishop." I said. "Thank you. You just can't know what this has done for me. I have to figure out a better way to integrate our families. Jacob's eighteen now anyway so he can see us when he wants."

"That sounds like a better idea than how you are going about it now. Is he in school yet?"

"He starts at Morehouse in a couple of months. He was up here with me going shopping and visiting the school when all that happened with JD."

"Oh… Well… Baby steps Jon. Go slowly with the integration is all I can say."

"I will," I replied as Janine knocked on the door. When Bishop opened it to let her in, I stood up, smiled into her beautiful face and walked out without a backwards glance. If he could help me see what I needed to do then I was sure that he would be able to help her bring her wayward self, back in line.

CHAPTER 23
Janine: On the Edge

The night after our second session with Bishop, Mishie called me sounding really off. I wasn't quite sure what was going on with her, except I could tell in her voice that something was drastically wrong. She wouldn't tell me what was wrong over the phone, so I told her I would walk over to see her. I felt bad because I hadn't been calling over the last couple of days like I usually would, but I knew if I talked to her, I would tell her what was going on in counseling. I didn't have it in me to keep a secret from her if she asked me what was going on.

I walked over to the house after I had fed Jon and Amber some of my infamous chicken and dumplings and put Amber to bed. I told Jon I was taking them some food and would be home in about an hour because I wanted to sit with Mishie a while. He didn't want to come, but told me to tell Marcus to come over to our house when I got there. I bought the food over in the crock-pot, so they could heat it up and eat it without any fuss.

Their kids had been sent to NY for a little while with Michelle's mom and dad because she wasn't getting any better and since it was almost summer and they would be in NY anyway, they felt it was best. I offered to take them a couple of times before school let out, but Mishie wouldn't let me, she kept saying, "You have your own fish to fry, girl."

I rang the doorbell, but it took them a really long time to come, then just as I balanced the crock-pot on my hip and was able to fish my cell phone out of my back pocket, Marcus came to the door.

"Hey Neene." He said as he swung the door open wide enough for me to step in with the crock-pot in tow.

"Hey Marcus, I bought you guys chicken and dumplings." I replied as I went into the kitchen, sat the crock-pot down on the counter. "I'm gonna plug up the crock pot and put it on high. It'll be hot again in about 10 minutes. You hungry? Jon wants you to come over, but I told him you guys may be hungry. Where's Mishie?"

"She's in the bed Neene. She hasn't been out of bed all week. They sent a hospice nurse a couple of days ago…" His voice trailed off.

"Hospice? It's that bad Marcus? What are they saying?" I turned to look at him.

"I don't know Neene, it's all bad to me. They're saying she may not make it through the summer."

I had to avoid his eyes completely. The tears they contained were threatening me, stabbing at my eyes until they too felt like they would start flowing a river that wouldn't be able to stop. "Is she eating? Think she may want a little chicken and dumplings?" I replied as I busied myself with bowls and plugs on the kitchen counter, turning my back to him completely to gather my tears and put them away. I couldn't face her with tears in my voice, much less on my face.

"She may Neene. I don't know. She hasn't been eating too much, a couple of crackers here and there, maybe some fruit. She hasn't been hungry really."

I finally turned and looked at him. His voice was trembling and his eyes were filled with tears that wouldn't fall. I had to attend to his grief, whether mine felt like it would drown me or not, "Marcus?"

He'd leaned his forearms on the black marble counter and looked down for a moment. He looked up and the tears that threatened to fall were now on his cheeks. "Neene. I'm really *losing* my wife. It's not like she's leaving me for another man or going away for a couple of weeks for work. She's going to be gone. *Forever.*"

"I know Marcus. I know." I said as I shook my head and rubbed his back. He laid his head on the counter and cried like a baby.

We stood like that. In his kitchen, while his wife – my best friend, lay upstairs readying herself to leave us both. After a short while, he stopped crying and splashed his face with some water from the kitchen sink. As he wiped his face with a paper towel he said, "Neene, man, I'm sorry for breaking down like that, but it's crazy. We've been talking about insurance policies all day and what she wants done when she leaves. The weight of it all is really heavy on me right now. Those chicken and dumplings smell real good, but I'm gonna go over and talk to Jon right now. I'll get some later."

"Okay, the door is open and he's expecting you."

He left me in the kitchen thinking about what was happening to our families. It seemed like my family's problems stemmed more from Jon's and my immaturity, but their family just seemed to be going through it for no reason at all. Why God did things like this to good people was what I really wanted to know. I know that rain falls on the just and unjust alike, but I just wanted this situation to not be so. I decided to pray a little before I went upstairs, *'God, it's me, Janine your servant again and I just wanted to come to you today to say thank You. Thank You God*

199

for not only allowing me to see another day but for allowing my friend, my dearest and closest friend, Michelle, to see another day as well. You are the great physician and can do anything but fail, so I know that if Michelle doesn't live through the summer, God, it's by your grand design and although I will be sad and my weeping may endure for a night, I know that Your joy will come with the morning light. That's how good You are God. If I keep my mind stayed on You, You will keep me in perfect peace and allow me to come into her presence with Your peace in me shining bright, so that she too can feel Your presence in this place tonight. I come to You tonight God, to ask You to extend that perfect peace to this family Lord, to touch them with Your healing hand Lord. To make their minds understand what their hearts already know Lord, that You are calling Michelle to be home with You. Not that it should break us, but that it should bring us all closer God, closer to each other Lord and closer to You, for You are Jehovah Rapha our eternal healer Lord. You are our guidance and Jehovah Jireh our protection. In this and all things, I thank bless and praise Your holy name. In the precious name of Jesus Christ I pray. Amen.'

By the time I finished praying, my face was wet with tears and my brow sweaty. I too splashed some water on my face and felt so much better. I was finally ready to go up to her room. Bishop told us that we need to pray more, that we weren't going to God as much as we should be for Him to intercede on our behalf and I decided when he said it that I was going to make sure I did that, if I didn't do anything else. I wasn't sure if I should take her some food, but I decided to take her a bowl upstairs anyway. My chicken and dumplings were her favorite so maybe she would at least taste it, if not eat a whole bowl.

The stairs creaked as I started up and Mishie called out, "Marc – is that you?" Her voice was low, and rough.

"No, it's me Neene." I replied, thinking maybe I should have brought her something to drink. "Do you want something to drink Misch?"

"Yes please," she replied.

I went back down to the kitchen and got her a glass of ice water in a glass with a few cubes of ice in it, like she liked it and left the food on the counter. I figured I would just tell her about it and see if she wanted some instead of just bringing it up.

When I opened the door, I was immediately struck with how small she seemed in the bed. She was a child in her mother's bed, swallowed up by fluff of comforter and mound of pillow. Propped up on several of them, her face was gaunt and her eyes, although bright, were sunken and surrounded by dark smudges.

"Here, Misch." I handed her the water with tears in my eyes.

"Hey Neene, thanks. I was so thirsty! Marcus was supposed to be getting the door and me something to drink like a half an hour ago. I thought it was Jon keeping him so long," she smiled and grimaced at the same time.

"What? Um... A...A...Are you alright?" I stammered.

"Yes! I'm okay, it's almost time for me to take my meds again though. What's that I smell? It smells like my auntie Joe's chicken and dumplings!"

"It is!" I grinned and then added, "I made it for you and brought it over. You wanna try some?"

"Yes girl! I want to taste it, at least."

I ran back downstairs thinking, "*Yes! Maybe I'll be able to get her to eat something...*" but by the time I came back upstairs, she was fast asleep. I got on the bed and lay next to her, but when I went to touch her arm and rub her back, all I could do was weep. She smelled metallic and felt like parchment dried in the sun, hot and dry – skin and bones both as fragile as a preemie.

She moaned in her sleep and began cry, so I tried to wake her, gently calling her name and asked her if she needed her meds. All she said was, "Marcus? ...I need Marcus, is he home yet? I need my husband Neene."

I jumped out of her bed and ran to my house. I started calling his name before I even got the door opened fully, "Marcus! Marcus! She's calling for you. Hurry! …I think she needs her meds." My voice trailed off with the last statement, because in reality I thought she was dying. Just then. I didn't want her to die without him there.

He jumped up from the chaise in the living room and rushed out of the house. I went to follow him, but Jon stopped me.

"Janine. Sit down baby, let them have this time."

I fell onto the chaise Marcus just vacated and began to sob uncontrollably. "What can I do? What can I do, Jon? What will I do Jon? She's really gonna leave me!" I wailed.

Jon just gathered me in his arms and waited until the tempest passed.

***

The next day, I went to work at Women at the Well, but it was rough getting up and going without knowing what was going on with Mishie. I asked Jon to call me if Marcus called him with any developments. They were in between projects now, which was a blessing; Jon got to spend time with Amber, while we waited for JD's release and Marcus got to spend time with Michelle while she was ill. This kind of thing rarely happened, so I know it was God. They would usually be working for months at a time with only a 2 to 4-day break a week. Suddenly, I thought, *'Although, with Jon splitting time between my house and Leslie's, it's no telling what their real schedules were all this time.'* I shook that thought off and said to myself, *'I refuse to dwell on that, I'm gonna thank God for them being home anyhow, because we are well taken care of and right now, we both need our husbands.'* I realized in our sessions with Bishop that it's not only *that* we think about what is going on in our lives: it's our *perspective or how* we think about it! I also learned that every thought that pops into your head doesn't have to take up residence; it just may be a trick of the enemy!

Jon called my cell phone right as I sat down at my desk with my lunch, "Hey, Neene."

"What's up Jon?" I sat my Subway sandwich down slowly, breathing jagged and closed my eyes, readying for the worst.

"Calm down baby. They are moving her to hospice care at Peachtree Christian Hospice in Duluth today. She's still with us though okay?"

"Okay," I exhaled slowly, "What are they saying?"

"Well, they are saying that they are going to have to give her food intravenously, so they need her to be in a facility. They are also saying that she needs her pain meds more regularly too. You okay?"

"No, Jon, but I... Did she send me any messages?"

"Just to come see her today, after work."

"Okay, text me the address. What are you and Amber going to do for dinner? I don't think there's enough chicken and dumplings left..."

"Don't worry about that Neene, I'll just take her to Chick-Fil-A."

"Good, she loves it there... Thank you Jon."

"For..."

"For staying... And for countless other small mercies you've given that allow me to grow into the wife you need."

"No need to thank me Neene. We're in this 'till death do us part." He replied then added, "I love you," before he hung up without waiting for my reply.

I went to the front office and spoke with Marie, our secretary briefly before I left to go see Michelle. I didn't know what to expect and after JD's hospital experience I didn't really feel too keen on going alone, but I made it there in good time. I played my favorite inspirational mix from my iPod on the way there; somehow Ledisi's song "Alright" and Yolanda Adams' "In the Midst of It All," have a way of making me feel able to face anything! The hospice was in Duluth on a really quiet stretch of land. When I pulled up, it didn't even have a hospital feel to it all, which I know Mishie appreciated having been a head pediatric cancer nurse all those years. She made sure her wing of the hospital looked more like a giant playroom for her pediatric patients than a scary hospital and this place looked like a resort more so than where people came to die.

I walked in to the lobby and was greeted immediately by an upbeat staff member with blue-white hair and a bright smile. She asked me whom I was there to see and said she would have someone come and escort me to the room. "Visitors tend to get lost sometimes because of the circular nature of the building," she chuckled. I didn't laugh, but I could see why. The place was kind of deceptive; when you first look at it from the front, it looks wide, but shallow, when you actually go inside you can see the depth of the building.

The stained glass and bright sun streaming into the reception area made it seem almost cheerful; that coupled with the fluffy couch I was sitting on made me feel like I was at a country inn somewhere. I could tell instantly that Mishie picked this place, well either that or Marcus really was the husband of the year! This had her written all over it; from the overstuffed chairs and fireplace, to the paintings and dark wood it was her style. I was the more modern of the two of us. She was a traditional girl. Always was.

A nurse arrived soundlessly at my side and startled me, "Are you ready? She's waiting for you."

"Yes, I'm ready."

She led me down a well-lit corridor, one side of which was almost all windows with paintings and bookshelves on the other side. We went past a small seating area and the nurses' station set in the recess of a wall that almost looked innocuous. Finally, we were at her room. I didn't want to go in yet. I paused trying to think about a way to delay going into the room and the nurse sensed it. She said, "I know it's hard to see your loved ones depart before your eyes, but we make sure they are comfortable and as pain-free as possible while they are here, so be at peace. Smile. She knows you're here and she's looking forward to seeing you."

I turned and smiled, but my throat had closed up with the tears I swallowed. I just turned the doorknob and entered the room. The sound of the IV machine was quieter than in any other hospital room I'd been in before, which was a miraculous feat because it had three bags of something pumping into her frail arm. She appeared to be asleep initially, but as I closed the door behind me, she opened her eyes. She was wearing a beautiful silk caftan of orange, white and turquoise with a matching scarf tied around her head. She was smiling, hard. "We're going out to the garden to sit and talk a while," she said while she swung her emaciated legs over the side of the bed and proceeded to hop down.

"Mishie wait, what about the IVs?" I rushed forward to help her, how – I have no idea.

"Girl. Don't worry, they move," she grabbed the IV pole away from my grasping fingers and wiggled it on its casters, adding, "I'm not as frail as I look!"

"If you say so." I laughed to myself and shook my head. She was more stubborn than I was once she got an idea in her head, but she looked a lot more vibrant than she did last night. I guess she really needed the intravenous nutrition and painkillers. We slowly walked down the brightly lit hallway bathed in sunlight from the floor to ceiling windows. A nurse appeared out of nowhere and asked if we were okay.

"We're fine. Just going out to sit in the garden for a few minutes. We'll be right back." Mishie said as we walked by her without stopping. Then she turned to me and said, "I just want to talk to you about my will and the kids and everything. I thought being outside with the flowers would make it... I don't know... Less depressing, I guess. Plus, those chicks are some gossiping some-bodies! They think I don't know, but I saw them listening to a patient's visit with the intercom on the last time I visited – Hmmph! They won't be spreading my business."

I chuckled, but felt strangely quieted. I wasn't surprised about the nurses' duplicity. The stories Mishie used to tell me about the gossipers and drama on her wing were hilarious. I not only didn't know what to say, I wasn't ready for this conversation at all; so, I steeled myself against the blows her next words would deliver as I followed her into the lovely garden. We went to a bench in the sun surrounded by pink and yellow flowers and she said, "I have approximately a month before I won't be able to breathe. The cancer has metastasized to almost all of my vital organs except my lungs, which is weird the doctors' say, but I say its God. He knows my big mouth has a few more things to say before he brings me home."

"What's on your mind?"

"Well, I want to make sure that you know I put a trust fund in place for Monique and Myles in yours and Jon's names. It's to be released to them when they've graduated from college, Marcus knows and the will is already in place. In the will it also says that if anything happens to him, that you and Jon are supposed to take custody of the children, but only if you are together."

"What am I supposed to say Michelle?"

"Maybe just that you are going to do it…"

"Of course I will take care of their trust fund, but Mishie you know as well as I do that my marriage may not last the week, so I cannot make any promises as far as that's concerned. It's not up to just me."

"I know Neene. I do… I just want you to understand that when I die, you and Jon are going to be the model for our children. They've been watching Marc and I closely, but once I'm gone, you will be the standard bearer. So even if it doesn't work out, I still need it to be where they can come to one of your homes and it not be a drama fest! You love drama Neene, always have. You were the Queen Bee from middle school all the way through college and you always had to have things your way. I thought that because I was the only one who could ever talk you down, that I may be the one you'd listen to now."

"Listen to you about what Michelle? I didn't come here to hear about how I need to keep my marriage together, I came to…"

"Jon was going to marry Leslie." She cut me off abruptly. My heart bled at the words, but then she dug the knife in a little deeper. "He knew she was pregnant when you two got married too, he didn't know she was pregnant at the time he proposed to you, but he talked to Marcus about marrying her right before you resurfaced from being with Robert. Men are different Neene. When they feel the time is right to get married, they get married and the woman that fits the criteria best – is the one who wins. You fit the criteria better than Leslie at the time, only because it wasn't just sex and looks with you, it was real love for him."

"So what! I don't care about all of that now Mishie. It's all water under the bridge now anyway. We shared everything about this already." My voice faltered ever so slightly. I really don't lie well; maybe I need to work on that, then again, maybe not.

"Yeah, but I know you didn't know he was going to marry her first. You better know that Leslie would do anything to get that man. She hasn't been married or even had a real relationship over the past nineteen years."

"How do you know all this?"

"Marcus tells me everything girl… You already know."

"So, Jon is telling Marcus this? That Leslie has been waiting for him? What in the world?"

"Not in so many words Neene. Just that she hasn't been married and that she was an eager ear and shoulder to cry on when you guys started having trouble a couple of months ago."

"Yeah well, Jon hasn't been back to South Carolina since JD's accident, so I am not worried about her."

"But he will once JD gets home and settled in good. Plus, he's going to have to resume work and traveling to those offices again sometime soon, because when I die, Marcus will not be good for anything for a little while at least. They can't leave the firm in the hands of the junior executives for much longer Neene."

"You're right. But what can I do? I'm already wrestling with the fact that this son of his is going to be in our lives forever! How do I control how that plays out, when I am not even part of the circumstance? Look Mishie, I'm supposed to be here to talk to you, about *you,* right now. Not this. Not now."

"You're right… I'm just scared to leave things unsaid and there's nothing left to say about me."

I grabbed her hand and said, "We don't need words anyway Misch. Let's just sit a while like we used to on our tar beach and watch the butterflies against the sky."

CHAPTER 24
Janine / Jon: Chickens Come Roosting

Janine

"Jon, come on honey! It's time to go pick up JD!" I shouted upstairs to Jon; he was taking his sweet time coming down and I was in hurry to see my baby boy back home. We had just finished up a therapy session the night before that was right on time! Bishop helped us navigate the forgiveness aspect, which was a decision that we both had to make and now we were on the mend.

"I know babe," he replied jogging down the steps towards me. "I was checking his room real quick to make sure everything is in place and secured for his weight." He came up grabbed my waist and kissed me softly on the lips.

"Oh, okay." I smiled softly at him in amazement. Last night was so sweet; making love was always the best part of making up. No one would have thought that we would be here after the hurricane we endured on the shoulder of I285. After we bared everything, every dirty secret each of us had held onto, some for way too long and others freshly painful, we realized that we could move on from that dark place and still love one another anyway.

In the meantime, we focused on loving up on Amber and on readying JD's room for his imminent arrival. Jon installed rails in JD's on suite bathroom, and I redecorated his room with lots of low-lying cushions and seating for him and his team to chill on when they come. He actually allowed them to come to physical therapy! It was great to see them all together, but now it was time to go get my baby and bring him home for good. This time in our lives has been incredibly difficult for all of us, but I think we may make it through after all.

"What are you thinking?" Jon asked me as I sat smiling, looking out of the window of his Escalade.

"Oh… Just about how blessed we are to have made it this far."

"Yeah," he grinned, "I'm happy we have gotten to this point myself. All of our cards on the table face up and neither of us has gotten up."

"Well, I guess we both left the table and saw that there was nothing better out there for us, then came back to the table knowing that what we needed was here all along," I replied.

"You just said something there, you know that?"

"Yup," I said grinning.

We pulled up to the hospital and Amber was asleep in the car, so I stayed in the car while Jon went in to get JD. I was glad about it, because I couldn't face seeing Kirk again. Kirk was the perfect gentleman that first week of therapy, but the sight of him helping JD unnerved me. The resemblance of Kirk to Robert, and JD to them both – it was too much for me to handle, so I opted to visit JD on the days when there was no physical therapy and let Jon take the other days. Now that I think about that, it may not have been the best decision, but it was the only one I had at the time.

I watched my husband go into the hospital and started to pray that when my son came out with him, that he would be of sound mind and body, ready to come home and heal. About fifteen minutes later, they emerged from the hospital's automatic doors and JD was walking on his own! The new prosthetic leg was strange to see him standing on, but he was steady and refused any help I saw Jon trying to give.

When they got to the car, I rolled down the window and said, "Hey JD! Wanna sit in the front with dad?"

"Nah, I'm good mom. I wanna sit in the back with Amber. Is she asleep?"

"Yup. You know she can't ride in the car for more than fifteen minutes without falling asleep! Something about her having to be still and the movement of the car just does her in."

He laughed and said, "True-life mom! I remember when we had to drive her around to get her to go to sleep when she was little."

"So... We have a surprise for you..." I said as I watched him finesse climbing into the backseat and kissing his little sister's forehead.

"C'mon Neene – You can't hold water! It's supposed to be a *surprise*," Jon said looking at me sideways.

"I didn't tell him what it was Jon dag! I was just..."

"You were just about to cave if he asked you more than two times, that's what you were about to do!"

All I could do was laugh, Jon was right. I was just so excited to have him home; I was bursting with all the things I wanted him to see in his new room!

"Alright, alright Jon, you win," I said finally.
"What is it Dad? What did you guys do?"

"You'll see when you get there. Patience JD, don't worry you're gonna love it!" Jon replied.

"Well, aight that's cool. I wanted to talk to you when I got home anyway."

"What about?" Jon stated turning to face him slightly as we stopped at a red light a few blocks from home.

"Patience dad," JD said and turned his face to the window.

All I could do was laugh, it was so good to see him cracking jokes and being the smart-aleck teenager he was before all of this happened. We had to attend a family session with a hospital social worker/therapist last week to talk about his release and how we should deal with him when he gets frustrated and down about what's going on with his leg and how different his life is now. They told us to treat him like he is whole; no matter what we do don't baby him, and to make sure that he has supportive friends come over. I was going to opt out of the session to be honest, I was tired of *seeing someone* about issues my family face, but I realized that spirit was the enemy trying to keep me away from the breakthrough that my son and family needs.

Jon

It was hard watching JD struggle to get it together before we walked out of those hospital doors. He didn't want his mother and sister to see that it was still difficult for him to walk easily with the prosthetic leg, but him pushing me away still hurt. Now, he's talking about he wants to *talk* to me when we get home… I hope he hasn't put two and two together and figured out that Robert is his father and I, unfortunately, am not.

I looked in the rearview and saw him with his head leaned on the window, asleep. He's always been a sucker for the car ride home, just like his little sister, no matter how macho he thinks he is. When we pulled up to the house, I parked in the garage and Neene took Amber to lay her down for a nap leaving JD and me alone.

"Hey. Hey JD. Wake up son." I said as I lightly tapped his shoulder.

"Huh? What? Oh dad... Aight. Nah dad, I got this!" He said as he pushed my hands away, stopping me from helping him down out of the truck.

"I don't know what your problem is J. Your mom is upstairs putting Amber down for a nap, so it's no one around but you and me. I'm not babying you, I just don't want you to hurt yourself dude."

"Look, I don't want your help man. I can take care of myself." He replied as he climbed down out of the truck, slowly getting his balance on his prosthesis.

"Really?" I said as I watched him attempt to get his bag as well. Shoot, I figured if he felt like that then he needed to feel how heavy that bag is then! That's almost 2 months' worth of gym clothes and underwear, plus sneakers – it's got to be heavy as all get out!

He grabbed the top handles and I stepped back, because I knew he was too unsteady to handle the weight of the bag and his own weight. As soon as I stepped back, he fell backwards into me and I caught him.

"Damn!" He yelled as he fell into me and the bag dropped to the floor with a loud thud.

"Watch your mouth young man. I don't know what's gotten into you – but I will say this, I'm your father and I am here to help you become a man, not to make you feel like you aren't. Remember that."

"Whatever." He mumbled as he slowly walked away from me and towards his room.

"What?" I replied following him getting angrier by the second. How dare his little snot nosed behind act like he has a chip on his shoulder with me!

"I just want to go to my room, *dad.*"

"Well, I can understand that *son,* but that is still no excuse for your behavior!"

213

"Really! C'mon dad, I just got back home from having my leg basically cut off! Does that give me a pass this one time?" He snarled turning to face me, his face in an angry grimace, and then shut his bedroom door.

When he said that, he looked exactly like his dad did when we first met. It was on the basketball court at school; I was whipping Robert's behind and he was so frustrated that he couldn't shake me to hit that 3-pointer – I thought he wanted to kill me. I stood in the hall outside JD's room stupefied. I couldn't even respond to his closing the door in my face. Neene walked up the hall, looking all excited and ready to show JD all the new features in his room and all I could do was look at her and say, "I just saw him in my son."

"Who? Wait a minute! Where? …Oh, Jon…" she paused. "What happened?"

"I was trying to help him out of the truck, but he didn't want any help. Then he tried to get the bag by himself and almost fell. I caught him, but he was really pissed. I don't know, Neene… It just doesn't seem like it's the same kind of pissed he was when he was in the hospital to me."

"I don't know what's going on either. Maybe we should give him some time alone? The social worker said he may be moody…"

"I'm gonna go in and talk to him for a minute first, then I'll leave him alone."

"If you think that's the right thing to do, go ahead. If you need me, I'll be in the kitchen." She kissed my face and squeezed my hand before walking back the way she came.

I stood outside the door to JD's suite feeling like a fool. I was afraid because I had no idea what my son was thinking and I just hoped that it wasn't I'm not his father. I figured anything else, I could handle. I opened the door and found him lounging on the pillows in front of his TV.

"What you watching? Can I join you for a few minutes?"

"Sports Center. I like what you guys did in here. It's really cool. I'm really feeling the posters and the arm thingies... Thanks dad." He said avoiding my eyes.

"What's up son? I'm feeling like there's something else going on and I can't let it go. You wanna talk to me about it?"

"Not really; not now Dad."

"C'mon JD. Your old man can take it. Spill it," I said bracing myself for this revealing of truth.

He paused for a moment, muted the TV, but continued to stare at it while he murmured, "I saw you with him."

"You saw me with who JD?"

"I saw you with him that day at Prime Town Center."

"What day JD? With who? – JD, I don't know what you're talking about!"

"I was driving home from my internship interview at Prime Town Center Gold's Gym. I met with the assistant manager because the manager was busy. I stopped at the corner and I saw you and him walking across the street. He had shopping bags like you had just taken him on a spree and you both were smiling and laughing..."

My heart stopped. I was in downtown Atlanta treating my son Jacob to a shopping spree, for getting A's and B's that semester after failing almost everything the previous one. It was all he wanted and I couldn't say no. It was the same day JD had his accident. I'd dropped him off to his mother inside the mall, right after we'd gotten lunch. Then, I headed over to Robert's office to talk to him about his investigation on Neene. This can't be happening. I knew it but I didn't know, couldn't handle hearing it from him.

"... I didn't know what to think, my brain started moving in slow motion and I just started driving. I never even looked up at the light to see if it was red or green, I just sped off. When the truck hit me, I thought it was the end. I thought that you all would just go on living with my clone and I would just be forgotten forever," He laughed absently. "Silly right? Who was that dad?"

JD stared at the muted TV; it was like he had retreated into himself and left a shell. Even the anger I felt from him earlier was gone. I felt like I had been gutted. The whole time I'm thinking about him knowing that I'm not his father, he's actually feeling betrayed by my being someone else's father. *How selfish have I been? How did I not see this?* I gathered my self-pity and threw it as far away from me as possible, said a prayer in my heart and mind to ask God to not only forgive me, but to give me strength to answer his questions calmly and with honesty. Then I replied, "Son, that was Jacob. He lives in South Carolina and came up with his mother to see me and for me to take him shopping."

"Why dad? Why? Weren't we enough?"

I gathered my son into my arms and held him; he allowed me to hold him, but was stiff and wouldn't embrace me. Then, I heard him begin to cry; a keening whimper that sounded like a wounded animal, then burst into a full–fledged monsoon of a cry. Snot and tears stained my shirt and his face was smeared with it when he raised his head from my shoulder and said, "Do you love us dad? Are you gonna leave us?"

"Never. I will never leave you and your sister. Daddy's not gonna leave you…" I replied as I too began to cry.

CHAPTER 25
Janine: Death Endured

When I got the call, I didn't know what to do. We had only been home about fifteen minutes, enough time for me to lay Amber down, go into my room to take off my jeans and put on a jogging suit. I went to see what JD thought of his new digs and was going to go jogging, but Jon wanted to talk to him alone. Then Mishie's mom called me from her bedside; she said Mishie had called out my name and her mother wanted me on the line so that Mishie could say goodbye.

Mishie came on the line breathless, "Neene, I love you like a sister, always will. Take care of our babies…"

Suddenly, her mother was back on the line, "Neene, we all love you girl… Wait a minute! I don't think she's breathing! Lord!" Immediately, there was a loud commotion with running footsteps, and a multitude of voices speaking at once. I heard someone call out, "CLEAR!" Then the line went dead. I sat on the edge of my bed with the phone in my hand for a full minute before I acknowledged what just happened. My best friend just died. I curled up into a ball on our four-poster bed and rocked myself while tears silently streamed down my face. I began to pray, *"Father God, I thank, bless and praise You for setting her free to be with You for eternity. She was an angel on earth and my voice of reason and although I'm sad she's gone from here God, I am so happy that she's finally free and there's no more pain... Please God help me get through this passing and take care of my only friend, in Jesus Holy name I pray. Amen."*

After a few minutes, I gathered myself enough to move and went downstairs to tell Jon. I wish my motives had been more about him knowing than about myself but honestly, I just wanted to be held. I went to the door of JD's room and stood there for a moment unsure if I should interrupt what I knew was a father – son, heart to heart, then I heard JD recounting what happened in his accident and was shell-shocked. He ran the light because of Jon! Jon actually had the audacity to bring his other family to Atlanta. I can't believe the gall of this man. *"Wait..."* I thought to myself, *"Did he just say he's never going to leave us? Well, I hope it's not because of guilt; I want him to stay because he loves us."* I slowly backed away from the door, deciding instead to let Marcus call Jon and let him know on his own. I wanted to confront Jon so badly, but decided to wait until after the funeral and everything had settled down a little bit. So, I headed over to the house to relieve the sitter and be with my godchildren until their dad and grandparents came home.

***

Helping Marcus and Mama Monique with the funeral arrangements had been taking its toll on me over the past three days. Mishie was the jokester; she could be brutally honest at times, but she always made you laugh no matter the situation and we ironically needed her comic relief at this very moment. As executor of Lil Monique and Myles' accounts until they were twenty-one, I was invited to the reading of the will, and we headed there with our hearts heavy and our minds on autopilot.

We found out that Mishie left an extensive will, along with a list of people she wanted notified of her passing that only Marcus could see. Being a pediatric nurse and the head of her department afforded Mishie the ability to save more than I imagined. My non-profit was just that – no profit, while she, on the other hand was able to save almost a hundred thousand for her children as well as leave them two hundred and fifty thousand from her insurance policy. She also had a separate policy for fifty thousand that she left to her hospital in a grant that would help refurbish the pediatric wing she worked in for fifteen years. Legacy building. My respect for her grew with every passing moment. When the lawyer said that I would be the one saying the remarks at her funeral, I almost lost it. I tried to say no, but Marcus asked me, "If you don't, who will?"

When he said that, I realized that not only was she my only real and true best friend, but I was hers as well and there was no one else who could do it. The funeral was to be at Wallace P. Williams Funeral home within reach of where we'd met our husbands almost twenty years prior. Our families had made small donations to both Spelman and Morehouse, so her untimely death and arrangements would be announced on their respective websites so that the lives she touched would be able to say their good byes and pay their respects.

There's something different about a down south funeral, there's more "to-do," pomp and circumstance and Mishie with her flair for that sort of thing, bought right into it. You would have thought she was born and bred in Georgia. The funeral had to be at Wallace P. Williams' funeral home because he was the only one with a white hearse and whose funeral home actually looked like a home in the Deep South, replete with overstuffed couches and the smell of home baked goodies, just like hers.

When we finally arrived at the funeral home I was tired. Marcus was tired as well. It was a good thing that

Mishie had pre-planned everything when she found out that her cancer was terminal. I thought she was being morbid, but I guess there were some benefits to knowing when you're going to die. All we had to do was hand the funeral home secretary the paperwork we received from the lawyer and she said, "Your beloved was extremely thorough in the details of her arrangements. Don't worry, she will be buried with the grace and style she was accustomed to and we will send Bishop Brown all the particulars. In the meantime, I suggest you work on the obituary and announcements to send to us. We will handle everything else. I believe you have a photo for me?"

"Oh… I almost forgot." Marcus replied as he reached into his jacket pocket and pulled out a photo and a thumb drive. "I wasn't sure if you wanted it to be soft copy or hard, so I bought both."

"We need the soft copy; the original should remain with you to be blown up for the poster by the casket as it will be closed. She didn't specify how many copies of the obituary she wanted for the funeral so I would need to know that before they can be completed. Take your time though; I understand it still needs to be written. Just keep how many you need in mind when you send the obituary to us so that we know. I believe that is all on my end. Would you like a short tour of the facilities?"

"No," we both said in unison.

"I need some air Marcus. I'll meet you outside." I quickly got up and left. I sat down on the porch out in front of the funeral home and rocked in one of the rocking chairs. I felt like everything was a dream. I talked to the kids that night and they told me that they knew their mommy had gone to live with God and that they should be happy, but they were really sad. They cried until their dad came home and then they cried some more. I couldn't take it anymore. I went home to find my house quiet; Amber was back in bed and when I went in to check on JD he too was fast asleep. Jon was in our bedroom stretched out across the bed with his bible in front of him reading aloud or praying when I finally made it upstairs to him.

He said, "I wish things had gone differently."

"You don't decide who gets cancer Jon. Only God does that and we know that we may not always understand his ways because they are not like ours. We just have to accept them."

"No, I'm talking about JD… About us."

That broke through my cloud of grief immediately. He was actually taking responsibility for what was happening between us. Wow. "I overheard about your being downtown and how JD seeing you with Jacob made him run the red light. I was shocked that you would bring them here and I have to admit I was angry as well, but Mishie stopped me from reacting the way I thought to initially. Even in death she was keeping me in check."

"I just wish I had told you about him in the first place. It wasn't as if I had been with Leslie since you. I didn't want to jeopardize our family, or lose access to my son if you found out about him."

"No. You didn't, but it doesn't matter. Our son will have to live with what's happened to him and we all have to deal with the fact that you have another family. I just wonder how it's all going to play out in the end. I feel like everything is spiraling out of control and there's no way for me to understand what's going on or why."

"I know I hadn't been being the best husband to you and even though I wasn't physically cheating on you with Leslie, I was emotionally cheating and in some ways that was worse. I just hope that you've really forgiven me."

"I don't know what to say…So much has happened, is happening…"

"I know, I just realized that in my role of husband, I just wasn't up to par with the standards I set for myself or even for you…"

"I most definitely fell short of the Proverbs 31 woman I appeared to be on the outside. I realize now that having the façade of perfection is nothing in comparison to having an authentic reality where we honor and respect one another. Although, my infidelity was based on some of my insecurities about us, it had more to do with my free will and choosing to do something I knew was wrong. I was immature and used you and your behavior as a way to justify what I was doing and it can't. It takes two to make a relationship right and Bishop is right in that we both have to take responsibility; you can't shoulder it all alone."

"You're right. Bishop is too, I feel guilty about JD running that light because I was with his brother. If I had done things right, he would have had a relationship with him and I know that I should have done better with us too."

"That guilt is a trick of the enemy! God doesn't want us to walk around broken down and hurting over things He's already forgiven us for – shoot for things He already knew we would do! We just have to confess our sins to one another ask for forgiveness from each other and God just like Bishop said, then the big job is letting it go."

"Yeah that, as well as not making the same mistakes twice."

"Exactly! Because we know I was headed down that road. Now we have to focus on getting Mishie buried in style and making sure Marcus doesn't lose it, which is all you Jon by the way."

"Yeah. I got him. About to head over there now, was waiting for you to get home so I could leave. See you in a little while; be back around 7-8 for dinner. Are you cooking enough for everyone? Can I bring them all over too? I don't think Mama Monique is up for cooking."

"They have more food over there than the law allows. Between Mama Monique's cooking all of the kids and Mishie's favorites, the nurses from the Pediatric wing, and our sorors, we're going over there for dinner to help them eat it all. Somebody just text me a few minutes ago asking what they need, because they'd made a pot-roast and some cabbage they were trying to bring over." I shook my head, "Honey, here in the south when somebody dies, people cook like there's no tomorrow. I'm about to text people back now to tell them to save their dishes for the repast at Wallace P. Williams after the service."

"Word? Well, that's one thing to be glad about! Good food is good food, no matter the occasion. I am going over there now, you wake the kids and bring them in a little while though, give me a chance to talk to Marcus for a minute first."

"Okay see you in a few."

As he walked out the door I was astounded at the growth we both showed in that one conversation. Had that been a few weeks ago, I would have been crying and upset right now and he would have been storming out of here about to tell Marcus all about it. Maybe it's true when people say that tragedy can bring out the best in people. I went down to JD's room to wake him and found him and Amber on the floor propped up pillows playing one of those games where they have to fling a bird across the sky to knock something down – they were cracking up, that is until they saw me.

"Are you okay mom?" JD asked.

"I guess… How are you guys doing?"

"I'm good mamma," replied Amber. "I just wanna know where they put Goddy Misch. I don't understand where she is now, I mean I know she has to have a funeral and be buried so that she can be with God, but where is she now mamma?"

"Goddy is already with God now baby," I said slowly, "She went with God as soon as her spirit left her body. Now her body is at the funeral home getting prepared for her funeral tomorrow."

"Oh… Okay momma… I understand," she said and looked at her brother like, *'I told you so.'*

"Mom, how are you holding up though?"

"I'm good JD. I came down here to check on you guys and you're checking on me! I'm just sad that we won't be able to grow old together and watch all of you guys grow up. That's the main thing that's bothering me right now. I have to remember that God's will is the way of our lives and no matter if I understand it or not, I have to learn to be content and at peace with it."

"What does content mean momma?" Amber said, turning her attention away from the flying bird on the screen for only a split second.

"In this case it means to be happy despite whatever is happening around me, even if I don't understand exactly what's happening or why."

"Oh, that's like when you tell me to do something I don't understand why for and I do it anyway, then it's like I was glad I did it because it came out great. Right?"

Both JD and I had to laugh! Little Amber's sense of logic is so wrong, its right. We headed over to Marcus' house, JD went to the den to turn on the game system, Amber went straight to her friends' room and I headed to the kitchen.

"Hey babygirl," Mama Monique said as soon as she saw me. "You hungry?"

It seemed like death just made people hungry and eager to cook for some reason. I guess the love people put into their cooking with their loved ones in mind help ease the pain and we all know good food can take your mind off of just about anything. Strangely, I wasn't very hungry maybe it was because my mamma was on her way here for the funeral. "Nah Mama Moe," I replied. "Maybe I'll get me something when I get back from the airport.

My mama's on her way down now. Her flight arrives in about an hour."

"When I told her she just broke down and cried. It was like she lost you. You know we loved you two interchangeably…" She shook her head and wiped her tears with a paper towel. "At first she was gonna ride down with me and Herman, but she needed to tie up some loose ends at the salon before she could hit the road."

"I thought she was gonna be with you guys when you came too. Her salon is doing so well right now, so I figured that was the hold up."

"Only your mother would retire and start a whole 'nother business! She always was a go-getter. You two took up right after her too. I was just a homebody, cooking and tending house…"

"Please Mama Moe! You're the reason we knew how to cook and clean a house! Shoot! I impressed Jon so good with my down home cooking, that he just *had* to marry me!"

We both burst out laughing, then it was like he heard his name the way he walked into the room. "Hey ladies. I smell some of those good collards and BBQ chicken up in here. Y'all burnin' it up! I know Mishie is smelling this in heaven happy that we are all about to break bread together as a family…"

Leave it to Jon. Sometimes, man… This guy just didn't know what to say out of his mouth.

Mama Moe just looked at him blankly and said, "It was her favorite meal, so I guess she is sitting back, probably taking it all in with a big grin on her face…"

"I have to leave go get mom from the airport. Be right back Mama Moe. Jon please make sure you check on the kids, they haven't come down yet and they all need to eat."

"Aight. Got it. See you when you get back." He said as he kissed my forehead and gave me a tight squeeze.

I left to get my mom with mixed feelings. She was always so critical of my marrying Jon. She wanted me to marry Robert from the very beginning and didn't really like Jon even after he afforded me the lifestyle she always wanted me to have.

CHAPTER 26
Robert: Funeral Crash and Burn

I heard Michelle died from one of my old Morehouse friends. I can't say I ain't like her, but I can't say we were ever cool either. I know she came with Neene to see me in court and I'm pretty damn sure she knew JD was my son, so I was going to pay my respects to her and Marcus, who despite his alliance with Jon, is still my man.

I decided to come strapped because I am a firm believer in being prepared for anything, plus I'm registered to carry concealed in this town, so why not. I pulled up to the spot in my Phantom and watched everything roll out; Michelle went out in high style and class. She had the white buggy hearse and I saw the workers with the white doves to be released at the end of it all too. I stayed in the background and watched Janine and that punk ass Jon come in with Marcus and what I guess was Michelle's mom and all of their kids right behind the casket. Every single last one of them was dressed in black, expensive labels apparent, but invisible at the same damn time. They all sat up front right next to the casket. I'd forgotten how rich these dudes were; Michelle was some kind of head of Pediatrics according to the news and the papers, so it shouldn't have surprised me that they were laced. I was kind of surprised they would have the funeral at ol' Wallace P. Williams' place, but then it was close to our schools and everyone was familiar, so it kind of made sense.

I sat in the back while Bishop Brown preached his behind off about how God never takes from us what we need and that if we just held on to God and not man, our lives would be less painful. I wish I could have received that word. It was a good one, but it fell on fallow ground with me. I'm one of those people who can't let things go. I sat there and watched when Leslie and Jon's other son arrived. I made sure I turned away when she looked in my direction, can't have her calling out my name and all that. She always was a groupie. Then I saw Jazzy from their clique come in with what I guess were her husband and children. I have to admit she still looked good too. The almost twenty years we'd been out of school had been kind to most of us.

I could smell the food from the repast from the back of the viewing room where the service was going on, so I decided to slip out and see what the ladies had cooked up for after the service. But as soon as I stood up, I saw Neene head for the podium and I quickly sat back down.

"Everyone who knows Mishie, knows me. That's just how we've always been. Ever since we were about 7 years old up until her untimely death this past week we've never had much time apart. We went to elementary, middle, high school and then college together and although our majors were completely different, even our careers were similar in that we cared for others in our daily grind. She was my most trusted friend and confidante, my encouragement when I needed to be pushed onward…" She paused and wiped her eyes and my eyes filled with tears for her pain. "…and the angel on my shoulder when I needed to be told to, '*Sat down girl*!'" As she would so eloquently put it when I was getting out of hand. I realize that I am going to miss her more than I thought today when I went to call her to tell her about her own funeral. Crazy right?" She stopped and chuckled then continued, "But she was the other half of my life outside of my husband and children, so it may seem crazy to you, but to me – it makes perfect sense. What does one do when they lose someone they invested almost their entire lives to loving? Do they die with them? Do they stop being able to love anyone else out of fear? Or do they love on? Love on despite the pain that may come if the person leaves. Love on despite the fact that we can't control what God's plan is for our lives. I say that when our hearts are broken open by the loss of a loved one, it leaves us open to love on. To love more fully and openly those who are still here to love us back. So today, when you leave this place after saying your goodbyes to this lovely angel who loved us all so well in spirit and in truth, go back to those who love you and love them with your heart broken open, spilling all the love it can. Thank you for coming to pay your respects to my dearest friend and sister. Please follow the direction of the ushers to join us for repast in celebration of her life."

I hopped up and got up out of there as smoothly as possible. I was dressed in all black Armani from head to toe with a crimson tie on for my crimson and cream; yeah, I was affiliated and proud of it. I headed to the repast room alone and with one eye over my shoulder just to make sure I wasn't spotted before I really wanted to be. I got me a plate and found a corner in the back of the room so I could peep what everyone was up to before I left just as undetected as I came.

"Hey Uncle Rob."

I looked up from my plate of homemade 7-Up pound cake to look straight into my own face. It was JD! *Talk about being spotted!* "Hey little man. How you feeling? You aight?"

"Not really, Mom's really sad and truthfully I miss Auntie Misch right now too. She was always joking; she always made everything seem better..."

"Well, you heard what your mom and the preacher said in there though JD, sometimes we won't get it, but we have to love who's left even harder."

"I didn't think about it like that Uncle Rob. Thanks..."

I sat my cake down on the side table next to me and stood up to give my son a hug. I couldn't believe he was almost my height, but then I was about his size when I was his age myself. I hugged him and he started to cry on my shoulder. I didn't know what to say so I just held him, patted his back and rubbed his curly fro.

Before I could say anything else to ease his heartache I heard, "What the hell are you doing here?" It was Jon.

"You act like this wasn't a public type funeral or like I didn't even know Michelle, Jon. Get a life." I replied as I slowly let JD go and stepped back. JD limped off slowly, looking back at us confused about what was going on.

"Yeah, you might have known her, but you didn't need to have your hands on my son. You need to get the hell up out of here right now."

"Is there really such a need for such hostility? I was just consoling my play nephew JD because he some kinda torn up about losing his Godmother, but I can leave right after I finish my cake and my conversation with my son. Oh – Wait! I mean my play nephew." I said coolly, looking Jon right in the face. It seemed like the whole room stood still and in retrospect I guess I deserved what came next, but I didn't expect it nonetheless.

Jon's right hand came at me so fast I didn't see it coming. The next thing I knew we were on the floor tussling and I went for my gun. On one hand it was instinctual, but on the other I really wanted this niggah dead. He had everything that was mine and I was tired of sharing. I felt like even if I couldn't have it, I wasn't gonna let him have it either.

I got my Ruger out of the holster and I heard someone scream, "He has a gun!" and pandemonium broke out in the repast. People started running towards the exit away from us, in the back of the room fighting for our lives. I cocked the gun but Jon was faster than he looked, he jumped on me, wrestling me for the gun. I got a round off, but it didn't slow him down, he still was able to snatch the gun away from me.

He stood over me with the gun in his hands as the police bust into the repast room, "Drop it! Drop it now or we'll be forced to shoot!"

Then I heard Neene's voice, "Don't do it Jon. He's not worth it. Please Jon… We need you."

When I heard that, I lost it. I rushed Jon headfirst, gun in his hand or not, this dude had to go down. When I heard the gun shot, I thought it was the police firing a warning, that is until I looked down and saw the crimson spreading over my cream handmade button down. This niggah shot me!

I heard the police say, "Drop it!" and the gun clattered to the ground.

They went to arrest him, but Neene's voice said, "Officer that gun belongs to the man on the ground. He pulled it out to kill my husband! Everyone here at the repast can tell you what happened, he was just defending himself officer. Look, he's been shot too!"

"We'll sort it all out at the station Miss. We have to take him downtown for questioning anyway. Where's my bus? We have a two-four-five with two wounded civs who needs attention STAT."

I saw the crowd, reporters and flashing lights as they wheeled me out to the ambulance and I have to say I was happy that Jon was being carted out in handcuffs in front of the media again because of me. Even if I didn't make it, it would be great to have his reputation destroyed by all of the negative media attention like mine. When I got to the hospital, I blacked out and when I came to – I was handcuffed to the bed, with a police guard outside my door.

CHAPTER 27
Jon: Vindication

This dude thinks he's slick, but I saw him when he pulled up in the rented Phantom. How are you supposed to be a detective and you're always trying to be so flashy? Whatever. I know he better not start anything at this funeral.

When my baby got up there she made me proud! I know Mishie was very proud of her too. I had tears in my eyes because I knew exactly how that felt to have my heart broken open, but to go on loving anyway. She didn't cry as much as she did when we went over it, which was good. I think it was flawless. Her mother decided to stay home and cook for the family because she didn't want them bringing any funeral home food back to the house and she didn't do to well at funerals. Thank God, because I couldn't take her side eyes and heavy silences, it was driving me crazy. It didn't help that Neene was grieving and there was nothing I could really do to ease her pain but hold her. My man Marcus was so distraught it was like he wasn't even there. Just hollow. Neene's mom went over to help dress the kids and get them ready for the funeral because Michelle's mom could barely get herself dressed. Neene wound up having to go over there and help them all because when the limos came, they still weren't ready.

I went over to the house to get everyone with JD and Amber because it was taking too long. I stuck my head into Marcus' man cave to see if he was ready or if he needed anything and found him just sitting in his study on the couch with his tie undone and his head in his hands, weeping, tears just streaming without a sound. I touched his shoulder and he started, but when he saw it was me, he was like, "Jon... This is more than I can take man. She's really gone. Her smell in the bed is almost gone. Dude. I can't..."

"Marc, man you have to. Your children are watching you for their cues. It's okay to cry and feel the pain, but never okay to give up. C'mon. Let me help you with your tie."

He stood up and allowed me to tie his tie because his hands were shaking terribly. I thought he was going to have a stroke or something the way he was shaking and breathing so labored. I said, "Do you need something? Want some water or something? You alright?"

"I need a shot of Patron Jon. Just one more, or some whiskey."

I looked at his desk and he had his bar emptied out onto it! "I don't know Marcus. This doesn't seem like a great idea man."

"Just one shot. It'll calm me down. I promise. Then you can take all the liquor out with you."

"Aight, just one Marc, no more than that. How many have you had today already?"

He sidestepped that question and hit me with this instead, "Take one with me; let's take one for Mishie – it's her favorite Patron, XO Cafe Dark. It tastes and smells like coffee so no one will be able to smell it on us."

"You know how me and Patron act up Marcus – You're tripping!"

"You only gonna have one shot fool, not the whole daggone bottle! Man, just one shot with your people before he buries his wife."

"Aight man. Dag. Alright… Look let's hit it and get up outta here before they come looking for us."

We took the shot in remembrance of Michelle and led the families to the limos so we could bury his wife.

After my wife said her peace, I gathered our kids, Marcus, Michelle's mother and their children, led the processional back to where the repast was being held at Williams'. We did things out of order because we didn't want to disclose where Michelle was being buried. We had the repast first at the funeral home, the burial was supposed to occur at 3PM, then we were going home for the dinner Jo was preparing and having partially catered, but I never made it home for dinner.

I walked into the banquet room looking for my son. Amber had come to me a few minutes before saying she couldn't find him and her mother sent her looking for him, because it was time to go to the burial. The staff was going to disperse the funeral goers with the releasing of doves, but we would be long gone. It wasn't like JD to disappear, so I thought maybe he was somewhere feeling down and I went to find him. When I saw Robert with his arms around my son, I immediately lost it. I don't know if it was the shot before the service or what, but the sight of the man who tried to tear my family apart with his arms around my son sent me into beast mode immediately! The reality of JD actually being *his* son never even came to mind.

"What the hell are you doing here? Get off of my son!" I grabbed JD away from Robert's embrace and told him to go find his mother.

He said something I wasn't trying to hear so I just said to him, "Look we all know you knew Michelle, but you really don't have to *still* be here. Especially talking to my son."

235

The next thing I heard come out of his mouth was him calling JD his son. I hit him with all of my might, knocking him to the ground and jumped on him before he could say another word. *'How dare him come here and say such things in front of all of these people?'* I thought, as I punched him and blocked his blows. It was bad enough that it was the truth in the flesh, but in the spirit, JD was all mine. I started pounding his face in and then I saw him reaching for something. This dude bought a gun to the funeral!

I jumped up and heard someone shout, "Gun!" Then all hell broke loose in the banquet room. Everyone started to run and push and scream, the tables full of food were overturned. Parents grabbed their children and high-tailed it for the door. I thought I saw Leslie scurrying out with Jacob, but I dismissed it when I heard the boom. He'd let a round off and it clipped me in the shoulder, but it didn't stop me from coming for his ass. I charged him and wrestled the gun away after some scrambling and fighting for it. I stood up, gun cocked and ready to take his behind up out of there, when I heard the police shout, "Drop it! Drop it or we'll shoot!"

I wasn't quite ready to do that. I figured if I take him out and they take me out, everything would work out eventually, but then I heard Janine's voice telling me that Robert wasn't worth it. That must have made Robert go crazy, because he rushed me and in the scuffle another round was fired, hitting him in the gut and making him collapse to the ground in a heap. I dropped the gun to the floor with a loud thud. There was blood everywhere it seemed. He'd shot me once through the shoulder and now his blood was pooling on the floor around him, mixing with mine at my feet.

The police seemed confused about whom to arrest at first. They took me to the squad car in handcuffs after the EMS came and patched up my shoulder. My wife was crying hysterically, I can't lie I wished I had taken him out for all the pain he'd brought me and my family. The news trucks were out in full force with their flashing lights and questions hurled over the yellow tape separating the scene in front of Wallace P. Williams' from the rest of the street. I couldn't believe it. I saw them wheel Robert out on a stretcher and take him away in an ambulance and God forgive me, but I hoped he didn't make it.

They took me to the station and I was forced to tell the police the entire story. At first, when they ran my fingerprints and saw the charges that Robert filed against me they thought that I was the perpetrator, but once I told them the whole story and the eyewitnesses corroborated that he was the one who not only bought the gun to the funeral, but started the fight and shot me first, they released me and the DA dropped the charges that he'd filed against me. I told them how he donated blood to my son at the hospital to prove that he was his birth father, how he was visiting him there without permission, how he was trying to get my wife to leave me and when she wouldn't, how he stalked and raped her on tape. It was difficult to get them to understand everything we had been through over the past three months and I thought I was going to have to be held until I could come up with the evidence, but they let me go after holding me for a couple of hours.

Janine was outside the police station waiting for me teary-eyed and tired, but when she saw me walk through those doors, the look on her face was priceless indeed. She loved me and there was no way I was going to let her go, no matter what.

CHAPTER 28
Janine: Life After Death

I woke up the next day still stunned with all that had occurred. The day before, when I'd gotten up in front of the people gathered to pay their respects to my dearest friend, I was happy to see that the last member of "le clique" was able to make it. Jazzy was still stunning and wearing her black with red and cream accents as we advised those closest to Michelle to do. Seeing her face in the crowd initially brought tears to my eyes. We hadn't spoken in over 6 months, but she was the only person I called aside from my mom when I found out. It seemed the more I backslid, the less I spoke to her or anyone else except Michelle, but I thought that was going to change after today. I saw Robert and I almost stopped speaking mid-sentence, but realized that he knew Michelle too and at least deserved to say his own goodbyes.

We had all eaten and Marcus and Michelle's mom had already put the kids into the limo to go and bury Michelle when all hell broke loose. JD came to the limo and told me that his dad and Robert were arguing in the banquet room; I told them to go ahead because I thought that things may get out of hand, I just didn't know how out of hand they were about to get. I called the police immediately though, because after Robert had Jon arrested and pressed charges to boot, I knew he was trying to do something to tear our family apart yet again and I needed to be one step ahead of him.

I thought I was going to lose my husband in front of my very eyes that day, either from a hail of police gunfire or from Robert pulling the trigger and neither was acceptable in my mind. I loved my husband too much to lose and had gone through too much to make our love work, to let anyone or anything stop us. So after they arrested him, I took a cab directly home and on the way called our lawyer Fitz, who told me to gather all of the evidence I could find and meet him at the station.

When I hit the door, my mother was all questions, "Where is everyone else? Why is your makeup so messed up? Where are you going?"

I gave her the briefest account I could so I could hit the door as quickly as possible to go and get my man – "Mom, I have to get my husband out of jail before our kids come home from burying their Godmother. Robert shot Jon and has been shot as well. I have to meet the lawyer at the station with the info to clear my husband's name."

"Oh, my Lord! What in the world has been going on down here? Go! Go hurry up and get whatever you have to get. If they get home before you, I'll cover for you guys... Oh Lord... Let me say a prayer... You just go ahead."

I heard my mother praying like I have never heard her pray before as I rifled through Jon's desk drawers and office safe gathering the CD Robert gave him and the pictures that Robert had of me working out with my PT, as well as the pictures from my safe of Leslie and Jon together in South Carolina that were all stamped with

240

the DDA (Douglas Detective Agency) stamp on the back. I even had some of the messages from Robert saved on my phone where he derided me, telling me that he would have me no matter what he had to do. I walked out the door as I hear my mother saying, "Amen," and I seconded that motion.

I jumped in my Lexus 450 and arrived at the station in 10 minutes flat. Our lawyer, Mr. Walter Fitzgerald was waiting outside in his black on black Bentley. I got in the back with him and gave him the sordid details along with all of the evidence he needed to get my husband out of jail, free and clear.

Fitz looked me in the eye and said, "Janine, don't you worry your pretty little head another second about this. By the end of the night, Robert Matthews will be in chains again and this time, he won't be getting out."

I sat in my truck outside that station last night, alternating between worrying about Jon's wound care and when they would release him and praising God for allowing him to still be here with us. When he finally walked out of the station, my whole soul cried out Halleluiah! I jumped out of the car and ran to him almost knocking him down in the process. He was so weak; he wobbled when I wrapped my arms around him.

"Ouch Neene!" he laughed a little and said, "I'm glad to see you too. I thought I was gonna have to walk home after all of this."

"Of course not! My husband – walk? Never. Not unless he wanted to walk the 10 miles back to the house with a bloody sling on…" I said walking to open the door for him on the passenger side. "You may have to hire a car service for a few weeks the way it looks now anyway Jon. Do you think we should go back to the hospital and get it checked out?"

"No baby, the paramedics said that the bullet went right through my shoulder. I just need to get some pain meds and to lie down. This dressing may need to be changed though," he said looking down at the blood seeping through the gauze.

"Okay. I'm gonna stop at the CVS on the way home and pick up some dressing for it and some Advil and Motrin and some peroxide..."

"No, no, no, no! Just take me home. I think we have that stuff somewhere in the house. Did they get back from the burial yet?"

"I don't know. My mom didn't call me, but she said she would cover for us though."

"Really? That's a first. Well for me anyway..."

"She was praying for you and everything so boy bye. Stop acting up! I'm so glad that you're coming home... I don't even know what to say."

"You don't have to say a word. Your face said it all when I walked out of the station. You love me and I love you more." He replied and closed his eyes.

We arrived back home right before everyone came back from the burial. I put Jon to bed and came back down to help my mother get everyone fed. The kids were hungry again of course, and all of the adults just wanted a drink. My mom, Uncle Herman and Mamma Moe wanted to know what happened with Jon and Robert so we retreated to the kitchen leaving the kids in the living room watching TV.

"Where is Jon honey?"

"Upstairs asleep. I gave him some pain meds and changed his bandages."

"What happened?" Asked Mama Moe and Herman in unison, while my mother's eyes widened in horror at the thought of the details.

"Robert shot Jon, and then Jon shot Robert at the funeral home after you guys left. I called the police and now Robert is going back to jail forever to make it short and sweet. Wait. Where is Marcus?" I asked realizing that he wasn't in the kitchen.

"He's over his own house; he wasn't hungry. He said to send Jon over as soon as he was able to come," said Mama Moe, then she asked, "Why would Robert shoot Jon? I thought they were friends from way back at Morehouse."

"Well," my mother said, "that crazy behind Robert never let Janine go, that's why! He must have been obsessed… I'm so sorry I even liked that fool."

I just shook my head and went upstairs to my husband. There was nothing else to say. With my momma there, I knew the kids would be bathed and put to bed.

I climbed into bed with my husband. I gazed at him in bed next to me and couldn't believe that with all we'd been through, our love had grown stronger than ever instead of withering and dying the way Robert thought it would. I turned on the TV, and then turned it up once I realized what was on:

This is Katie Hollis of Atlanta's WSB-ABC and I am reporting live from outside of Wallace P. Williams' funeral home where the illustrious philanthropist and Spelman graduate Michelle Johnson was laid to rest earlier after succumbing to pancreatic cancer. However, the service ended in anything but a peaceful celebration of her life. Robert Douglas Matthews of Douglas Detective Agency was rushed to the hospital in what seemed a life threatening gunshot wound and Jon Dupont, who it seems was also shot, was taken into police custody – Back to you in the studio Jenn.

Thanks Katie. Well, we now know that there will be no charges filed against Jon Dupont, but Robert Matthews, who is no stranger to run-ins with the police, will be charged with a litany of accusations ranging from assault with a deadly weapon, inciting a riot to stalking and even rape! This is a case that will confound many who are old enough to remember the best-friend rivalry that these two shared while at Morehouse. Robert went onto the NFL and shortly thereafter was arrested on a series of drug and solicitation charges while Jon went on to build most of Atlanta's newest and best-loved infrastructures. We are not sure what happened, as the exact details are sketchy at this time, but we do hope that the Dupont and Johnson families are able to mourn the passing of their beloved Michelle Johnson without any further strife.

I sat there dumbfounded at how quickly this story was all over the news and the insinuation that there was more to be discussed made me worry about whether they would let it go. Disgusted, with my stomach actually turning, I turned off the TV and crawled back under the covers, spooning Jon being watchful of his shoulder wound. It was the safest and happiest I'd felt all day, as a matter of fact it was the most content I've felt, *ever...*

EPILOGUE
A New Day

Janine rolled over and immediately had to throw up. The stomach flu she had gotten from the kids just didn't seem to want to go away. She ran to the bathroom with one hand over her mouth and the other on her stomach pissed knowing she was about to throw up that good shrimp dinner and grits and eggs she'd made in the past twenty-four hours.

As she kneeled over the porcelain bowl, Jon came in and rubbed her shoulders saying, "Baby, I think you need to go to the doctor, it's been almost two weeks of this and the kids are better already. We don't need you to be dehydrated and passing out at work. Have you been able to hold anything down?"

"No. *Urgh!*" She retched and moaned, "I just want to go back to sleep now Jon. I don't even want to think about going anywhere right now."

"Okay. I'll take the kids to school and call the doctor for you. When I get back, we are going to get dressed and go to the doctor's office, so be ready or at least be ready to get ready!"

Jon got the kids out of the house and came back as quickly as possible. He was working in the Atlanta office, while Marcus worked in the South Carolina office this week for the first time since Michelle's death. All of the kids were staying at Jon and Janine's, so he had to go across town to a high school, then come back and go to elementary school nearby to drop them off (it started later), which one would think gave Janine ample time to get dressed. Unfortunately, when he came back, she was back in bed, fast asleep with crackers and tea on the nightstand, and the black duvet over her head to block out the morning sun.

It had been two months since the arrest and conviction of Robert Matthews on all counts, but Janine hadn't been right since right before the funeral. It started with the loss of appetite, which was expected with the great deal of stress she had been under with her best friend's death and the pressures of dealing with the aftermath of her wayward behavior. But the nausea, vomiting and weird cravings were all pointing to one thing – she was pregnant. The only question now: Who's the father?

The Wayward Wife

Wife

A Novel

By Tanefa Wallace

A BOOK CLUB GUIDE

ABOUT THIS GUIDE

The following questions are suggested to help your book club conduct an in-depth discussion on The Wayward Wife and offer some alternate perspectives to what the story offered as one woman's truth. We hope that you are able to find some new and interesting angles and are able to enrich your conversation and enjoyment of the book.

BOOK CLUB QUESTIONS AND
TOPICS TO DISCUSS

1. What did you think when they learned that JD was not Jon's son at such a critical time?
2. What would have been your reaction if the nurse told you that your blood didn't match your son's when he needed a transfusion?
3. How do you think Janine dealt with the exposure of her indiscretions? Did she?
4. If you were Jon, would you have left Janine immediately when you found out she was cheating or went the PI route?
5. Janine goes into therapy against her will in this novel. Do you think that therapy was a viable option for her?
6. Do you think African-Americans obtain needed therapeutic services when they should?
7. Why do you think African-Americans hold a stigma against talk therapy?
8. How did the thread of child molestation running through the book affect your reading?
9. How do you think her childhood traumas contributed to Janine's behavior, if at all?
10. Many of the main characters are Christian, and very active and visible in their church; were their personal lives a surprise? Why? How?
11. How do you think the relationships Janine and Jon shared with their respective best friends affected their marriage?
12. Is allowing other's input into your marriage advisable? Even if they mean well or know you well, do you think their advice should be used to inform your relationship? Why/why not or to what extent?
13. Which character would you say provoked the strongest response from you? Why?

14. Robert seems so determined to get Janine back in this novel! What do you think drove him to such lengths to get Janine back?
15. Which character do you think changed the most from the beginning of the novel? In what ways?
16. The Wayward Woman is mentioned in the bible as a woman to be avoided at all costs (Proverbs 7 and Proverbs 23: 26-28), the bible doesn't, however, give an account of how these women became that way, think of Gomer – Hosea's wife (Hosea 1, 2, & 3) and the Samaritan woman (John 4:16-18). This was part of why this novel was written – Do you think that Janine is a representation of how a woman can become wayward? Why?
17. Did you think that Christians were perfect or strived to be? Do you think this book does harm to the witness or view of Christians and Christianity?
18. What about those Christians who have fallen and gotten back up like the ones we have met here – Are they accurate depictions of people who love God, but are flawed?
19. Which one of the men is the father of Janine's newest child? Why do you think he is the father?
20. Do you think there should be a sequel? Where would it go if the story continued?

FOR NEWS AND INFORMATION ON
UPCOMING BOOKS FROM T. S. WALLACE
FOLLOW HER ON THE FOLLOWING SOCIAL
MEDIA OUTLETS

WEBSITE:

www.TanefaWallace.com

BLOG:

www.TheWriteWayFaye.Wordpress.com

IG:

@TheWriteWayPub

FACEBOOK:

https://Facebook.com/WriteWay